O9-ABH-414

Also by Kathe Koja

headlong

KATHE KOJA

headlong

FRANCES FOSTER BOOKS
FARRAR, STRAUS AND GIROUX
NEW YORK

Copyright © 2008 by Kathe Koja
All rights reserved
Distributed in Canada by Douglas & McIntyre Ltd.
Printed in the United States of America
Designed by Jay Colvin
First edition, 2008
1   3   5   7   9   10   8   6   4   2

www.fsgkidsbooks.com

Library of Congress Cataloging-in-Publication Data
Koja, Kathe.
  Headlong / Kathe Koja.— 1st ed.
    p.   cm.
  Summary: High school sophomore Lily opens herself to new
possibilities when, despite warnings, she becomes friends with "ghetto
girl" Hazel, a new student at the private Vaughn School which Lily,
following in her elitist mother's footsteps, has attended since
preschool.
  ISBN-13: 978-0-374-32912-9
  ISBN-10: 0-374-32912-5
  [1. Friendship—Fiction.   2. Boarding schools—Fiction.
3. Schools—Fiction.   4. Social classes—Fiction.   5. Family life—
Fiction.   6. Orphans—Fiction.]   I. Title.

PZ7.K8296Hea 2008
[Fic]—dc22

                                          2007023612

Acknowledgments

Thanks to Amy Hand, Scott Hedges,
Phyllis Kendrick-Wright, and Janet Kurowski
for the interviews. Many thanks to Karen Hand,
Beth Holland, and Eric Linder for enthusiasm and
welcome. Special thanks to Carla Young and
Laura Lamberti, above and beyond.

And as always, thanks to Rick Lieder,
Chris Schelling, and Frances Foster.

To Jane, Deborah, and Denice

h e a d l o n g

1. June

A black circle-in-a-circle-in-a-circle, a bull's-eye, a target: I trimmed it from the symbol sheet, painted on glue, stuck it to the underside of the vestal's upraised wrist, one of the few blank spaces left on her. Decoupage, a French word, or from French anyway: *découper*, to cut. My vestal was kind of plain, compared to other people's, all bald and smooth and monochromatic, neat black symbols glued on white plastic skin. Hazel's was just a head, a Styrofoam wig form mounted on a toy plastic police car. Mrs. Parais gave her a zero for materials, but extra credit for presentation and creativity.

"That'll dump your final grade," Audrey said, satisfied. Audrey had done hers with ribbons and magazine cutouts, totally pretty and forgettable, like some mannequin in a mall.

Hazel looked at her, then at me, and shrugged. "I'm not worried."

I was running late with my vestal. She was due on Thursday, our next-to-last full day in the next-to-last week in the year. After that was Convocation, and then we were done. It was June, the public school kids were already out for the summer, clumped up at Starbucks, laughing and shoving. The girls looked younger than we did, somehow, or freer. Like the girls in Hazel's neighborhood, with their Jessicka jeans, tons of lipstick like kids playing dress-up. As if they were less—serious than we were. Less something.

The bell sounded for third period, but I didn't leave. The room was quiet around me, the long clean worktables, papier-mâché vases and flowers, some lower-school project waiting to be picked up. A twist of paper stuck to my infinity bracelet, my hands smelled like glue. The symbol sheet had so many cutouts it was turning into lace. At the bottom was a row of little wheels, or flowers, captioned *growth, rebirth, confusion, renewal*. I cut out one, a seven-armed wheel, blunt black with an empty white center, and stuck it carefully over my vestal's right eye.

Fourth period, I had already passed my swimming final, so I was free. The walkway to Peacock was empty at this time of day, you weren't supposed to go back to your room during class hours. "Hazel?" I said. She was stretched out full-length, all five-eleven of her, hair pulled back, eyes closed. The sunlight shone through the green ash trees, a spangled kind of light, as if we were underwater. It was cozy there, the bricks held in the heat.

"Hazel?"

"Mm."

"Are you asleep?"

Silence.

"Are you—"

She half opened one eye. "What?"

"Nothing."

"*What.*"

"Are you—" Are you Bone, or Lady Vaughn? Are you my best friend? "Are you going to dinner with Edward, or what?"

She yawned, wide and pink, like a cat. "No. I don't know. . . . I'm going to sleep. I *was* asleep," play-shoving my leg, closing her eyes again. The ash leaves flickered. Her head against my thigh was heavy and warm.

2. September

A million potted white and yellow mums, bundled corn shucks, ropes of fake autumn leaves; every year the Mixer committee seemed to decorate more. I was at the punch table with Kells, my boyfriend; his real name was James Keller but everyone called him Kells. I did, too.

We'd been back to school for three weeks, settling into classes, the year's new routine, so everyone had already seen each other, really. But the teachers kept encouraging us to "mix," because it was Welcome Back Mixer, where you were supposed to rove from dorm to dorm, Peacock to Crane to Cormorant to Kingfisher, drinking punch and meeting all the new people who weren't actually new at all, most of them you'd been seeing for years. Especially if you were a lifer, like me.

I'd been going to Vaughn—the Vaughn School—since pre-K, as a day student; I was an upper-school sophomore this year. My mother had gone to Vaughn, too, which made me a kind of double lifer. My dad went to Lamb. . . . I knew that some people called us the "Vaughn Virgins," like we were untouchable or snobby or something, but that wasn't exactly true. Yes, we were all very focused, especially the upper-school girls, but was that so bad? School is like a mini-life, that's what the teachers were always telling us. You do well at Vaughn, you do well at Harvard or wherever, you do well in life. That's the expectation. That's how it works.

Now "Let's go over to Crane," Kells said in my ear. "Patton's got some choice smoke, he said."

The common room was filling up, everyone laughing and talking. Hazel Tobias stood by the door, alone, chewing on a cookie square. "She's in my Lit class," I told Kells.

"Who is?"

"That girl there."

"The punk rocker one?"

She did look kind of punk-rockish: so tall, impossibly thin in impossibly tight black pants, tire-rubber sandals, some kind of wire bracelet, her tiger-streaked hair pulled back. At Vaughn, people—girls—were into a very classic kind of look: ballet slippers and hoop earrings, Tiffany charm bracelets (the charm bracelets were especially big that year, even a few of the teachers had them), round black sunglasses, that kind of thing. I didn't have a ton of charms on my bracelet—just a heart-and-anchor, from my parents, and a butterfly from Kells, *for your butterfly kisses,* he told me—but I still wore it. So Hazel looked really—different.

In class she was different, too, Ms. Holzer's Lit class,

we were doing reading logs for *Franny and Zooey* by J. D. Salinger, picking either Franny or Zooey to follow through the book. Hazel started in on Day One—or Day Eight, really, she came to class a week after the rest of us—arguing with Ms. Holzer: *Well why does it have to be only Franny or Zooey? There's Mrs. Glass too, Bessie. Or Buddy Glass—*

Ms. Holzer liked to act really friendly, like she was just one of us girls, but she didn't like to be argued with; she wasn't used to it. *Franny and Zooey are the main characters, Hazel, they're the ones we're going to—*

Why can't I be Seymour? Hazel said.

Nobody knew what she meant, except Ms. Holzer, who frowned: *That's a totally different book,* but Hazel wouldn't give up, they went back and forth, people were watching it like it was a tennis match. Finally Ms. Holzer sighed and said, *See me after class.*

That night, before I did any other homework, I sat down and flipped through the book until I found Seymour, page fifty-two, in a footnote: *the eldest of the Glass children, Seymour*: he commits suicide. I thought that was a little odd. Why would she want to be someone who wasn't even in the book?

Hazel was still by the door alone as Kells and I walked out. I smiled at her, but she didn't see me. All over campus, the paths and walkways were lined with luminaria, flickering like fireflies. When we walked into Crane's common room, Patton waved us over: "Hey Lils, gimme some sugar, girl. Kells, man, you will love this shit. It's phenomenal."

In their common room, at the punch table, Mr. Haywood and Edward Flowers were passing out cookie squares. Mr. Haywood waved us over, bumped knuckles with Patton and Kells.

"Going to be a great season this year, guys. Maybe state finals?"

"Absolutely, sir," Patton said. He rolled his eyes at Kells. Edward Flowers watched, a half smile on his face. We followed Patton downstairs, through the yellow-tiled laundry room, the smell of old fabric softener, out into the dusk behind the dorm, the long damp lawn that led to the evergreens and the river; it was getting chillier, now, you could feel that it was fall. I shivered, and Kells put his arm around me.

"This will knock you on your ass," Patton said. He pulled out his chunky lighter, puffed, passed the pipe and "Hey," someone said out of the dark, a girl's voice I didn't recognize at first. Then she came closer, up the slope from the river path, and I saw that it was Hazel Tobias.

"Anybody got a cigarette?" she asked.

Patton took out his pack. They were face-to-face over the flame for a second, she was just as tall as he was, which was unusual. Very few girls could see eye to eye with Patton.

"Well hey," he said, in his talking-to-girls voice: a little drawly, a little—superior. I didn't always like Patton very much, but he was Kells' best friend, and he was one of the phenomenal guys at Vaughn, chair of the Student Leadership Committee, captain of the hockey team, 4.0, all of that. And he was hot, too: tall, and blond hair that he was growing out to his shoulders, pale gray-blue eyes. Everyone said he could be an actor if he wanted to, just because of his looks, he could easily be in the movies or TV. "I'm Patton Ponder," he said to Hazel, like he was delivering essential information, which in the context of Vaughn he actually was.

"Patton?" Hazel said. "After, like, the war movie guy?"

"No. After my dad. And his dad."

She didn't say anything. She seemed—not unimpressed, but not aware that she should be impressed, like Patton Ponder was Joe Blow was John Doe and that was nice and so what. I felt myself smile in the dark.

Patton looked at Kells, then back at Hazel. "You want to smoke some pipe, or what?"

"No thanks," she said, and left, just like that, just walked away with the cigarette, back down toward the river. No one said anything for a minute, until "Weird," Patton said. "Weird girl."

"If Haywood catches her smoking," Kells said, "she's in deep shit."

I didn't say anything.

• • •

When I got back to my room—just after after eleven, I was a sophomore now—I went online for a while, then checked my mail; there was an e-mail from my mother in my inbox. Nothing urgent, just *How was Mixer?* She was keeping in daily touch, or trying to, but I didn't always answer right away.

It was our compromise, my parents' and mine. At the end of last term, I had talked about maybe looking into the Open School, or Europe or someplace; they suggested—my mother suggested—that I try boarding for a year instead. My dad had been—not angry, but baffled. Well, angry too. He didn't like things that he couldn't understand.

Why would you want to leave Vaughn, Lily? What's the problem?

There's no problem.

Then why would you want to leave?

I didn't know how to answer him, really, I wasn't even sure that I wanted to leave. I didn't hate Vaughn, hate being there, or anything, I just wanted to try something—different. So I shrugged, and he turned to my mother: *Is this about some boy, or something?*

Being in the dorms was a little different. I knew all the day student group, like Julia Baumgarten and Keisha Robinson and all of them, but I was friends with Alondra LoDuma, too, and Devi Gupta, and Greer Reinhardt, I'd been to their room parties in Peacock, so it wasn't a huge stretch to move in there. And Mrs. Alwin, the dorm mom, had promised my mother she would look out for me specifically: *I'll keep my eye on Lily, Mrs. Noble,* she said when they brought my things. *I know she'll do well here.*

Lily always does well, my dad said.

Across the room, cocooned under her giant pink Risa Rice comforter, Constance Brill was sleeping, making that damp snuffling sound she made: not snoring exactly, more like a dog dreaming; I think it was allergies. It wasn't that bad, but right then it was enough to keep me from wanting to go to bed. So I let myself out into the hall, I didn't need a key, we weren't allowed to lock our doors. The hallways were quiet now, only a few rooms still had lights on. I ended up downstairs, in the common room. Hazel Tobias was there, sitting on the floor by the French doors, eating a cookie square. She looked up when I came in.

"Hi," I said.

She was wearing a funny long nightshirt, a man's pink-and-gray-striped nightshirt, the sleeves reaching over her wrists. Her shoulders looked like a coat hanger, like a model's; she had model cheekbones, too. Sitting like that, her back so taut and straight, she reminded me of some kind of sculpture, of Lady Vaughn, actually, the Greek goddess statue at the school entrance, standing there with her bow drawn, arrow aimed at Success.

"Where's General Patton?" Hazel said, but not like she wanted an answer, or expected one. I wondered if I should ask if she wanted company. She didn't seem to. Finally,

"Are you just going to stand there, or what?" she said, so I sat down.

She smelled like cigarettes, and something else, something sweet; incense? She had a little pile of cookie squares beside her. "You must really like coconut," I said.

"I hate it, actually, I just didn't have any dinner. I got there too late, or something. And your cafeteria sucks."

"The dining hall? Why?"

"Well for one thing," she said, breaking a square in half, "there's no hummus. Or hot dogs. And no line. . . . You know," impatiently. "Just those—islands, or whatever they are."

"You mean the hot station, the sandwich station, all that? What's wrong with—oh. You mean you had servers at your other school?"

She made a face. "No, we had a *line*, with trays, and plastic sporks. And long tables to sit at, not stupid round restaurant tables. . . . Servers, *god*."

I had no idea what she was mad at, if she was mad. "Where did you go, before here?"

"Trust me, you never heard of it."

"I might have. Was it Brookside, or Spence, or—?"

"It was Bertram. Bertram High School. I told you you never heard of it." She relaxed back a little, leaned her head against the wall. "A line in the cafeteria, a *lot* more brown people, and a much, much lower population of BBGs."

I decided to ignore the remark about brown people. "What's BBGs?"

"Burberry Bitch Girls. No offense." She pulled a cigarette out of the nightshirt pocket.

"You can't smoke in here."

"You can't smoke *anywhere* here, apparently, but you know what? I'm going to anyway." Opposite the French doors were three narrow windows, kept locked at night, everything was locked up at night, but somehow she got one open without tripping the alarm. She lit the cigarette, blew the smoke out the gap. Cool air drifted in. "This is going to be difficult," she said.

"How did you—"

She reached down into the window groove, and fished out a tiny piece of plastic, bent just right, just the width of the corner between the window frame and the window, and wiggled it between her fingers. "Works on doors, too. Some doors."

I smiled; I didn't know why. "That wasn't difficult."

"I meant smoking in general, here. Duncan said I should just quit, he *expects* me to quit, but—"

"Who's Duncan?"

She didn't answer. Then we heard footsteps coming down the hall, medium-quick: Mrs. Alwin. We both froze. Hazel jerked her cigarette hand out the window, ready to ditch, until the footsteps passed.

We didn't speak. She finished her cigarette, and I just sat there breathing in the night air, the smoke, feeling the quiet of the room, the dorm, all that quiet and just the two of us here awake, until "Why do you like Seymour?" I asked.

She stared at me. Narrow brown eyes, dark eyebrows pulled together; I felt my face turn pink.

"In *Franny and Zooey*, I mean. Why do you want to be Seymour, instead of—"

"Because Seymour's not there," she said.

I didn't know what to say to that. I didn't know what to say to her. Do you know how unusual that was, for me I mean? My entire life, I'd been around people that I always knew exactly what to say to, and what they would say to me, and what I would answer back. This was so . . . different.

She was still looking at me. "What's your name?" she said.

"Lily Noble."

She didn't say anything, her name, anything. Finally "I'm going to go to bed," I said.

"Me too." She stuck the plastic prop back into the window frame, locked the window again. You could still smell smoke, but very faintly. "See you in *Franny and Zooey* class," she said, "unfortunately. No, I mean—I don't mean you."

"I know," I said. And I did know, I wasn't just saying it. Whatever she was mad at, it wasn't me.

She hid her crushed cigarette butt in half a squished-up cookie square, wrapped it in a napkin, stuffed it into the trash. Slipping out of the common room, she turned right, a tall pink-and-gray shadow; I turned left. The light was on in Mrs. Alwin's office, I could hear voices, whoever was AOD that night; it sounded like Mrs. Parais. No one heard me. Constance Brill was still making her dreaming-dog allergy-noise; she didn't wake up when I closed the door.

Before I went to bed, I answered my mother's e-mail, *How was Mixer?* I wrote, *I had a good time.*

In Ms. Holzer's class the next day, she spot-checked our reading logs. There was a lot of grumbling, and Audrey Zhang got semi-hysterical when she realized she'd left hers back in her room, and would get an automatic zero.

"But I did the work! I had like *four pages* written, I read up to page *twenty-six*—"

"Audrey. Everybody." Ms. Holzer held up her hand; her charm bracelet jingled. "I told you all that I'd be doing spot checks, I told you that there were no excuses for not having your log with you and up-to-date. Pass them in, please."

Audrey was still bitter about it at lunch, saying what a bitch Ms. Holzer was: "Now I'll have to do extra credit work just to jack my GPA back to normal, and I have like two papers due tomorrow—"

Julia rolled her eyes. "God, stop complaining, Auds." She was calling everyone "Auds" and "Lils" and "Als" like Patton did. They'd had a quick thing last year, a nano-fling just before summer, so ever since school started she'd been trying to hook back up with him. So far it wasn't working. Last night, at Mixer, he'd been with Alondra, but that would never go anywhere, Alondra was too much of a flirt. "It's just one stupid zero, let it go."

"That's easy for you to say."

Around us, our table, the lunchtime buzz, a hundred girls' voices rising and falling; sophomore year was the last segregated lunch, next year was coed and everybody ate in the boys' dining hall that was twice the size of ours. Almost all of the tables were full, except the one right next to the kitchen doors that everyone avoided; sometimes some of the kitchen workers sat there. Our table was by the window. Next to me, Audrey pecked at two spoonfuls of garbanzos and some lettuce, telling Keisha that she had to lose three pounds to get back to a size two. Someone else said, "Did you ever see Lori's mom's vanity plate? It says SIZE 2."

"Oh right. *Lori's* a size four."

"Her mom drives, like, a Volvo or something."

"My mom said she'll buy me whatever I want when I get my license next year."

"I have got to lose weight," Audrey said.

Alondra sipped her ice water. "I heard if you eat only baby food, you can lose like five pounds in two days."

"That's total bullshit," Keisha said. "Baby food is the most fattening food of all. It's for *babies*, to help them grow, not get thinner."

Julia nudged me. "Where were you last night? I didn't even see you."

I sipped my apple smoothie. There were tiny chunks of apple in it that kept clogging the straw. "I was there. I went to Crane with Kells." Suddenly calling him "Kells" seemed silly, like Julia calling Audrey "Auds." Why don't I just call him by his name? I thought. Why don't I call him Keller? Or James?

Extra casually, Julia asked, "You saw Patton?"

"Just for a minute."

"Who was he with?"

"*You* should know," Keisha said, nudging Alondra, who made a theatrical little shrug, half smiling and "I was with him for like five minutes," Alondra said. "It's not like we had *time* or anything. . . . Anyway Olivia was there, too."

"Oblivia, you mean?"

"Julia, god, you're so mean."

"Well she is, she's practically special needs—"

"I heard she got implants over the summer."

"No, that was Alicia. Olivia's are real."

Past Alondra's shoulder, I caught a glance of something tall and quick: Hazel, wearing the same black pants but a different shirt, a man's tailored shirt, white with yellow striping, the sleeves cuffed back to her elbows. She crossed the dining hall, past the hot station and the salad bar, to the sandwich station, said something to the server there, a heavyset black lady who smiled at her, but she didn't get a sandwich made. She took an orange from the fruit bowl and stuck it in her bag, a big bulgy slouchy kind of DJ bag crisscrossed with peeling blue duct tape. Most people, girls, had Burberry totes. *Burberry Bitch Girls.* I had one, too, but my mother had gotten me a Peyton tote for this year, monogrammed. . . . Hazel was heading out of the dining hall already. On an impulse, I waved. She saw me, and stopped. I waved again, the wave that means *Come here.*

"Who's that?" Keisha asked.

"She's in Lit with me," I said, *see you in* Franny and Zooey *class* but we hadn't talked there, we sat at almost opposite ends of the horseshoe. I did notice she'd turned in her reading log.

Now she stood behind my chair, arms crossed, far enough back that I had to half turn to talk to her and "Come sit with us," I said. "There's room." Devi scooted over, and after a second, Hazel pulled an empty chair from another table, where the Korean ESL girls sat, folded herself into it and set her bag down between her feet. "Did you eat already?" I said, which was stupid since I'd seen she hadn't, it was just something to say. Everyone was looking at her. "This is Hazel," I said. "That's Devi, Keisha, Alondra, Audrey, Julia."

They all said hi, various kinds of murmurs and polite little noises. Seeing Hazel with my friends was such a contrast, like in art, what Mrs. Parais calls "juxtaposition," putting things side by side to highlight their differences. Like they, we, were all girls, all Vaughn Virgins, but other than that—

Alondra put her head to one side; her dangly gold earrings swung. "You're in my Web page class," she said, "aren't you."

Hazel took the orange from her bag, dug her thumb into the fat peel. She wore the wire bracelet again, some kind of woven metal, silver and green. "I'm in Web design, yeah. With Mr. Downtown Brown. Kind of a stupid class."

Alondra snickered. Julia and Audrey glanced at each other. "Why do you call him that?" Keisha asked.

Hazel shrugged. "Because that's how he acts, like he's all downtown and hard-core, with his spiked earring, and music, and everything." The orange smell was sharp and sweet. "He probably lives in a gingerbread house."

Alondra giggled. "He lives on campus," she said to Hazel. "Over by the duck pond." And then they laughed together, and for just a second I felt—I don't know, annoyed, or—I don't know.

Then Hazel pushed away from the table, hoisting her bag again and "I gotta go," she said to me. "Where's the Student Accounting office?"

Alondra said, "It's in the—"

"I'll walk you over," I said, getting up.

"Nice to meet you," Julia said, making her second-best Student Leadership smile. Sometimes I wished she would just, you know, give it a rest. I knew she dreamed of herself and Patton as First Scholars, king and queen of the school, riding off to Harvard together in the sunset. Which was fine, but I sometimes got the feeling that to Julia, we were all extras in her movie, hers and Patton's. Which was not really my definition of a friend.

As we left the dining room Hazel asked, "What's that one girl's name? The Latina girl?"

"Alondra? She's Spanish. Alondra LoDuma. . . . Go this way," as we turned from the dining hall to the main hallway, the main entrance doors with their mosaic design, a fan pattern, blue-and-ivory letters—the Vaughn colors—radiating out from a central golden sun: REASON—KNOWLEDGE—INDUSTRY—SERVICE. Hazel's long striding legs, I matched my steps to hers, those funny tire-tread sandals and "Did you do your reading log on Seymour?" I asked.

"Yup. Seven pages."

"He kills himself, doesn't he?"

"Not in that book." Sun came bright through the trees, the leaves just starting to melt into their fall colors; some trees had red and green leaves at the same time. Hazel dug around in her bag, pulled out a big Ziploc. "I'm starving. You want some of this?"

"What is it?"

"Gorp. Good Old Raisins and Peanuts. Like trail mix. . . . You never had it?"

There were walnuts in it, too, and pumpkin seeds, and tons of dark-chocolate chips. It was delicious. We each took another handful. "It's good. Where do you get it?"

"Duncan always—Magnus—I brought it from home."

When she frowned, her whole face frowned, eyes, chin, everything. Who's Duncan? I wanted to ask. Who's Magnus? But "I was almost late to class this morning," she said, deliberately changing the subject. "I had to go back and change, Mrs. Alwin said I couldn't wear my No Exit shirt. 'No logos or slogans,' " she mimicked, sounding like Mrs. Alwin, the slurry way she talks sometimes, no-logos-or-slogans. "Not unless it's like *Yale*, or something. Or *Vaughn*. You sure have a lot of asshole rules here."

"Didn't your old school have rules? Bertram High?"

"No, we had metal detectors."

"Why are *you* acting all downtown and hard-core?" and Hazel laughed, a different laugh than before, like she was surprised, I had surprised her; I was smiling, too. "Do you secretly come from a gingerbread house, or something?— That's the Admin building," approaching its stone steps, the pockmarked stone flowerpots on either side spilling carved roses and apples—Symbols of abundance, Mrs. Parais told us once. "Student Accounting is on the first floor. I'll go in with you, I need to top up my card anyway."

The Admin building was one of the oldest things on campus, built in the 1920s or something; they always show it on the tour, to impress new parents that Vaughn has history behind it, and outstanding architecture. The lobby was like a setting in an old movie, domed echoey ceiling, glossy checkerboard floor, frosted glass doors and "See you," Hazel said, turning toward Financial Aid. I'd never been in there. Disbursements was where you put money on your debit card; you said the amount you wanted, and they made a charge to your account. Your parents' account.

Kells was in Disbursements, leaning on the counter, his eyes squinty-pink. He smiled when he saw me. "Hey, babes. Lils-babes."

"What'd you do," I murmured, "smoke your lunch?" and he laughed, a kind of silly laugh, raked back his hair with his fingers. He was growing his hair out like Patton, but his was fuzzier, curlier, a wavy sandy brown; it didn't look as perfect. Nothing about Kells was quite as perfect as Patton.

He put his face close to mine, one hand touching me, low, behind the counter so the Disbursements lady couldn't see. "Can I come to your room, later?"

I smiled. I didn't really feel like smiling. Smoking always made him silly, like a nine-year-old. A sex-obsessed nine-year-old. "I don't know. I've got a ton of work."

"Ooookay," and he wheeled around, whacking his backpack into the door, the lady at the desk looked up and "Your card," she said, pointing. "You forgot your card." She was an older black lady, maybe like my mother's age, in a white blouse and blue-tinted glasses; she sounded kind of tired. For a second I wondered what it might be like to sit behind that desk all day, handing out money to kids like Kells; did she look at him, them, and think, *spoiled rich kids*? What did she think when she looked at me?

The door banged shut behind Kells. "Can I help you?" the lady said.

"Yes, please," I said. I made sure to smile.

The little Japanese light was on over my bed, making a cozy pink glow; I liked to do my homework there, propped up by pillows, not at my desk, which I mostly used as a storage area. No reading log tonight, since Ms. Holzer still had them, but I did the reading anyway, up to page twenty-six, where Franny talks about how she can't really stand the people she goes to school with; I knew Ms. Holzer would want us to comment on that. She likes things that have resonance in your daily life. I still had geometry homework, and a project due in Urban Patterns, but most of that was just going to be PowerPoint, so that would be easy.

Schoolwork wasn't a huge worry for me, or at least not the way it was for some people, like Audrey, who did nothing but complain, or Constance Brill, who seemed to procrastinate, then panic. Mrs. Dixon, her adviser, gave her a little motivational sign to help her focus: a tiny cartoon guy staring up at a giant mountain, with "It's Not As Big As It Looks!" underneath it. To me, it should have been the opposite, a big guy staring down at a little mountain, but either way it wouldn't have helped Constance. Her desk was a tornado of sticky notes and scribbled-on papers and empty water bottles and things with parts missing, like a scale model of her mind. Mrs. Alwin said she was from some kind of magnet school, so you'd think she'd have some skills, but apparently Vaughn was unhinging her. . . . She wasn't really a bad person, but she was a bad student, I mean she didn't seem to know how to *be* a student, she didn't know how it was all supposed to work.

There was a lot of pressure to do well at Vaughn, a lot. Not just to do your best, anybody can do that, but to succeed, to get the numbers. People calculated their GPA every day, several times a day. Vaughn was all about "achievement," and you learned, you *had* to learn, how to do it. Not how to know things, no one ever talked about that, knowledge, but how to get an education, be the best. Even Kells and Patton, all the people who liked to party, they never let it mess up their grades, or if it did, they found a way to balance things out with extra credit work, or snuggling up to the teachers, volunteering for one of their pet projects or something. And if you hadn't learned how to do that by middle school, you left. Or you ended up like Constance Brill.

Right now she was hunched over her computer, trying to get some new program to load, getting more and more frustrated; you could feel it coming off her like waves of heat. In a minute she would be asking me for help, to do it for her, so "I'm going downstairs," I said. "Want me to bring you something back?"

"A new brain," she said. She sounded clogged and mournful, like she couldn't breathe through all her problems, her allergies and overdue papers and misery. The year had just started, how could she be so behind? I was starting to wish I'd chosen my own roommate, and not let Mrs. Alwin pick for me.

Going into the hall was like escaping into fresh air. Nearly all the room doors were open, laundry bags humped up beside; you left your bag out on Tuesdays, and they picked it up. Or you could use the laundry room, I guess. All the doors were decorated, with yarn flowers, glitter stamps, pictures, posters, stuff torn out of magazines or the *Vaughn Victor*: people playing sports, or declaiming in class; you could put up your friends' pictures, but not pictures of yourself, unless you were with friends. Otherwise it would look like bragging. People bragged all the time, of course, but there was a right way and a wrong way to do it: you had to act as if it was no big deal, like you *expected* yourself to do well, that you were happy but not surprised when you did something spectacular. . . . So much of Vaughn was about that, about doing things the right way, the best way. Being the best.

Music floated through the hallway—we couldn't have movies or TVs in our rooms, but we could play music, not too loud, or Mrs. Alwin would come by and make you turn it down. She was in her office, talking to one of the freshman girls, patting her back, like *there, there.* I looked in as discreetly as I could, to check my cubby and see if I had mail; Mrs. Alwin gave me a kind of *must you?* frown, but she didn't say anything, and the girl didn't even notice me. On the floor below the cubbies was a package, creamy purple-and-white, marked FRAGILE. It had Hazel's name on it.

Downstairs, the common room was warm and noisy, the French doors were open to get a breeze. A couple of freshman girls were watching a movie, some Pakistani ESL girls crowded around the refrigerator, a big bundle open on the main table, food from home or something. Hazel was in the corner in a club chair under the CLEAN UP AFTER YOURSELF! sign, feet up, reading a skater magazine. *Franny and Zooey* was facedown on the floor beside her.

"Hi," I said. "You got one, too."

"One what?"

"A package."

She squinted up at me. "What kind of package?" so I went with her to get it, Mrs. Alwin alone in the office now, giving us her measuring smile: "What's up, girls?" and Hazel ignoring her, scooping up the purple-and-white box, out the door as "Lily?" Mrs. Alwin said, so I stopped, I had to and "Are you and Hazel Tobias friends?" Mrs. Alwin asked, coming around from behind her desk.

I nodded.

"She needs a friend." There were tiny little stains across

the front of her Vaughn T-shirt, little drops of something shiny, greasy; her glasses were spotted, too. "I think you could be a very good influence on her, as long as you keep in mind your own experience, and your own values."

What was that supposed to mean? "I will," I said.

"I'm sure you will. . . . I've told your parents how well you're adjusting to dorm life." She was smiling, now.

"Thanks," smiling back, back to the door and out into the hall, Hazel was waiting for me and "Come on, Good Influence," she said as we headed up the stairs. "Bring your good personal values, won't you?"

"I have no idea what any of that was about," I said, embarrassed, and annoyed at Mrs. Alwin; Hazel was smiling, a snarky kind of smile, but not at me. What *was* it supposed to mean anyway? My "values," what was that?

Hazel's room was at the stairway end of the hall, its door totally bare except for a magazine picture taped dead center, a girl wrapped in layers of bandages, like a mummy, or a burn victim. All you could see were her eyes, big and scary-blue. Inside was just the opposite, pictures stuck up everywhere, the walls, the closet, the bathroom door, even the ceiling, pictures of buildings and streetlights and gang-looking kids on corners, kids with their mouths open, a girl shirt-up and flashing from a taxi window and "Wow," I said, trying to look, to see all of them at once. "These are, they're phenomenal. Where did you—"

"Hold this a second," she said, handing me a little razor-blade tool, making space on her bed for the package—one bed? I hadn't even noticed, with all the pictures. "You have a single?" I said. "*Wow.* How did you get a single?"

"My—I requested it. *Crap,*" picking at the package tape, I gave her back the razor tool, turned around and around looking at all the pictures, some of them from magazines, some printed out: a few big, most small, two very small ones taped to the wall beside her bed, of the same two people, two guys, one with short hair and a big sunny smile, the other dark and super tall and unsmiling, he looked exactly like Hazel: her dad? Too young. Her brother, then. In one picture the two guys had suits on, the brother had his arm around the smiling one; in the other they were in swimsuits with a fat little black-eared dog between them, standing on a deck or dock or something, water behind them sparkling white and blue and "Who's that?" I said, pointing. She ignored me. Was she ignoring me? "Hazel? Who's—"

"Finally," she said, digging into the box. "He wraps it like it's going to Mars. . . . Oh, good," pulling out a bright red package, CHERRY HOT ROPES, "he got the big one. Want some?" ripping into the bag of licorice, a huge bag, the smell of cherry filled the room as she emptied out the box: a couple more skater magazines, a bundled-up yellow anorak, a little Ziploc full of hair; hair? and "From my dog," she said, seeing me look, backhanded-tapping the picture of the two guys on the dock, the dog. "Elbow."

"Elmo?"

"El*bow*. He sheds on everything, year-round." She

opened the bag and sprinkled the hair on the floor, on her bed, laughed when she saw my expression. "*Now* it's my room. . . . Don't you have a dog?"

"No, I—we never had any pets. My dad— No. Why is his name Elbow?"

"I don't know. Magnus named him. Maybe it means something else in Swedish. Here," pushing the licorice at me, "have some," but "Who's Magnus?" I said, looking at the pictures by her bed, thinking now that I knew and "Him," she said, in a sour kind of way, tapping the smiling one. "That's Magnus, OK?"

"Don't you like him?"

She stared at the floor, a clump of the dog's hair and "I love him," she said. "You know, could we just not talk about our fucking families, OK?"

"OK," I said, but I had to ask because now I knew, her brother and Magnus were partners, and she was self-conscious about it, maybe people had been mean to her or something because her brother was gay, but I wanted her to know that I was absolutely not like that, it didn't matter to me if someone was gay or straight or whatever so "Just tell me," I said. "Is that your brother with him?"

She made a noise, half-exasperated, half-angry, tried to say something but started coughing instead, choking on the mouthful of licorice, she coughed so hard I got nervous and went into the little bathroom for water, tubes and towels and bottles everywhere, I couldn't find a glass but "It's OK," she called, still sounding a little strangled,

"I'm not dying. . . . Yes that's my brother, Duncan. Duncan and Magnus and Elbow, on the good ship *Sink or Swim*, la la la." She coughed again, seemed less mad, got up and "Just a second," into the bathroom to drink from the sink, trickling water and I saw on the picture closest to me, ripped out of a magazine—two boys, skater boys with an old black man between them, very dignified, suit and tie and hat—and slanted red letters at the bottom: *Duncan Tobias knows the streets.*

Duncan Tobias. Hazel Tobias. Magnus Tobias? And Elbow. *Our fucking families.* My family, the Nobles, Philip and Helen. And Lily. No dogs, cats, pets, siblings. No boats. No care packages, but lots and lots of e-mail. No pictures, either. Why was that? I didn't have a single picture of my family in my room.

I took a strand of licorice and wound it around and around my finger, chewed off the tiny sticking-out end. Hazel hopped back down on her rumpled bed, pushed at the empty box with her feet, the purple-and-white box, "Music to Your Ears" in curly script across the side. "Magnus gets it at this place uptown, the Sweetheart Shop, they have all kinds of weird candy there. I got hooked on it when I was a little kid. . . . It's hot, isn't it? Wild cherry and jalapeño. Not everyone can take it."

It *was* hot, fiery and sweet, and I loved it immediately, like I had the taste for it before I even knew it existed. "It's phenomenal," I said. I unwound the rest of the curling strand and stuck it all in my mouth.

Debra Alwin

What sets Vaughn apart, I think, is the quality of our girls. We do draw from all over, all over the world, really, girls from every kind of background, girls for whom English is a second or even third language, girls for whom Vaughn is a major life experience. That is, I would hope it is that for all of our girls, a major experience, but some girls have more of a transition to make than others.

We strive to give each girl what she needs individually, whether it's extra tutoring, or a little boost in settling into dorm life, overcoming homesickness, or whatever she might need to make her time here happy and productive. I do think it's important for the girls to be happy. I have always believed that we learn better, we live better, when we are happy.

Some girls are definitely more of a challenge than others to settle in. While we modulate our admittance standards to ensure a diverse student body—because we are very proud of our diversity, our very diverse student body—a full twenty percent of our girls are on scholarship, and then there are the Wilmington scholars as well—but blending in all these different kinds and classes of girls can take some doing! Not every girl arrives with realistic expectations of what Vaughn can provide for her. And not every girl is the right girl for Vaughn. Some very nice, very brilliant girls actually do much better elsewhere. We are always sad to lose them, of course, but we recognize that to be a Vaughn student is not the right fit for everyone. You can often tell, early on, who these girls are.

As with any quality school, there can be a certain—I wouldn't say "resentment," but an expectation of, of clannishness, of— Such as calling the upper class girls "Vaughn Virgins," as in, I suppose, vestal virgins, girls who are set apart from the others. I think this is a very unkind and unfair way to categorize our top girls, who work very hard to be both excellent students and fine young ladies. I don't mean to be unkind myself when I say this, but I believe that's just ignorance talking. And perhaps a little jealousy, too. We are very, very proud of our top girls.

3. June

"Hello?"

"Magnus."

"Lily?" That musical voice, the pleasure in it, wild barking in the background. "Hey, Calla Lily, how are you?"

"I'm fine," I said. I had a damp washcloth draped over my head, my bare feet up on the windowsill. The breeze smelled like the river, murky, almost metallic, alive. "It's getting really hot here. . . . Wow, what's wrong with Elbow?"

"Nothing. The pizza guy's just leaving. How're you doing, girl?"

"I'm—" I closed my eyes. "I wish I had some pizza." I pictured Magnus, phone cradled on his shoulder, opening the pizza box as Elbow danced around begging, like he needed any more calories, the little porker. He was supposed to be on a strict diet, only special low-cal food from the vet. "Do you want to eat? Am I interrupting you?"

"No, no no no. Talk to me."

So I did. Feet up, head back, I draped my face with the

washcloth, and talked: about trying to finish my vestal, about Convocation, about getting an eight for my swimming overall, when it really should have been a nine, about Kells and Audrey almost getting caught hooking up: "They were practically right out in the open," I said. "Not too bright, huh?"

"You sure that's not bothering you? Those two?"

"No. Not at all." And it really didn't, except that it was a little strange to think that Kells was doing all the things he used to do with me, to me, to Audrey now, as if we were basically interchangeable. Audrey had those flavored condoms in her bag, Tropical Passion, it made me laugh a little. Kells and Auds. . . . But I wasn't mad at either of them, why should I be? It made perfect sense, Julia and Patton, Audrey and Kells, the lead roles and the understudies, they all belonged together. But not me. . . . If I had another boyfriend, I wouldn't have noticed them at all, probably.

"So, did you talk to your adviser-lady?" Magnus asked.

I shifted. The washcloth slipped sideways, letting in the sunlight glare. "Not recently."

"You know what I mean. About next year. You told me—"

I closed my eyes again. I imagined we were sitting at the kitchen counter, Elbow staring up, flicking his ears every time one of us reached for a napkin or a glass. And Duncan somewhere in the background, working, sorting through pictures. And Hazel—

"I mentioned it to her, yeah. She gave me some places to check out."

"Well?" I didn't say anything. "This is a big decision. Did you talk to your parents or anything? . . . What about Hazel, did you talk to her?"

I didn't say anything.

"Calla?"

I didn't say anything.

"Lily—"

"I know," I said, even though I didn't, which was why I couldn't talk to Hazel, or my mother, or Ms. Nell. Or Magnus, even. Or myself. "I will. Just— Don't be mad at me, Magnus, OK?"

He made a breath, gentle, exasperated. "Mad at you? Oh stop. I could *hit* you, yeah, I could cut you off your Cherry Hot addiction—"

"Don't you dare, don't even *joke* about—"

"Cold turkey, clear your head. . . . You're going to do the best thing, I know you will. You just have to find your path."

All of a sudden there were tears in my eyes, warm and prickling, I squinted them back but more came welling up. Anybody can be nice to you, that's easy. Being kind is different. "I know," I said. I had to clear my throat and say it again: "I know. I will."

"Now will *you* be mad at *me*, if I go let this dog out, before he has some kind of seizure, before he—"

I laughed, half crying. "You're going to give him pizza,

aren't you? Don't lie. You big pushover, you can't say no to anyone, can you?"

"Only myself," he said, and laughed. "That's hard enough. . . . Take care, Calla."

"You too," I said. As I reached to put the phone back on the nightstand, I knocked the gendarme doll onto the bed, loose rag doll legs and arms, zipper up his back. He smelled like the river, too.

4. October

"God, I barely finished," Keisha said. "I spent all night working on the dance." She pulled her Urban Patterns book out of her locker, stuffed a fat blue folder inside. The lockers at Vaughn were extremely tiny, people said, but to me they seemed just right, just enough room. Besides, most of your stuff was either in the dorm if you were a boarder or in your tote if you were day, so you didn't actually need a locker anyway. Keisha was day; her tote was always crammed full.

We started walking to Lit together. "How come you're not on the dance committee this year?" she asked me.

"Um, I don't know." I didn't want to be on the dance committee. The year before I'd been on the holiday committee, and I'd had a headache every single day. Dealing with the lower-school Penny Partner drive, the mothers on the Parents' Council calling me every day, what does any of that have to do with anything, really? Even Vaughn? "Are you chairing it?"

"Co-chair. Patton roped me in. And Edward Flowers.

That is one sexy boy, Edward Flowers, have you ever noticed that?" She made a kissy face. "I sit next to him at the meetings. We *discuss* the *agenda*."

Down the main hall, the vine-patterned carpeting, past the millions of plaques, the posters for Brown and Cornell, the Craft Department's showcase—yarn sculptures and hangings, god's-eyes and Shaker loops—past the ladies' room and the teachers' lounge and "We picked New Horizons," Keisha said, because the Halloween dance was always a benefit dance, the ticket price went to charity, and there was a Best Costume contest that you had to pay to enter. Plus people from the charity were always invited to the dance, if they wanted to come. In freshman year it was the Humane Society and they brought in some shelter dogs; *that* was fun. Some of the dogs even wore costumes, like little devil horns, or sparkly tutus. I wondered if Hazel ever dressed her dog for Halloween. Elbow.

"What's New Horizons?" I asked.

"It's like for girls who have babies. . . . Did you do your thing in PowerPoint again? I made an animation this time."

Walking into Lit, I could tell right away that Ms. Holzer was in a pissy mood, tapping her nails on her desk, she almost never sat at her desk. As soon as we were in our seats—I was on the window side of the horseshoe, next to Hazel—she told us how disappointed she was because "I really expected you guys to get this assignment," she said.

"That's why I chose the journal format in the first place, instead of just question-and-answer, or straight essay. I really expected you to run with it." She started passing out the reading logs. "But obviously you haven't."

I got mine back with a 72. I'd never gotten a 72 on anything I'd ever done at Vaughn, even in the lower school. I could feel my face getting tight. No one said anything. Hazel bounced her pencil very quietly against her leg. Her log, I saw, was marked 98.

"In fact, there's really only one person who's gotten into the spirit of the assignment. I won't name names, she knows who she is. And *you* know by looking at your grade whether or not you need to put more effort into your logs, more of your self." Ms. Holzer blew a breath through her nose, a vastly irritated sound. "Now. We're going to discuss the phone call Zooey makes from the spare room, his brothers' old room. Why do you think he calls Franny like this, when they've just been sitting there talking in the living room? Greer? What do you think?"

"I think," Greer said, "that I'm glad that I don't have any brothers or sisters. Actually the whole book makes me feel that way."

Hazel started doodling in her log, looped circles and stars. The Cherry Hot wrapper was sticking slightly out of her backpack. As soon as the bell rang, I reached into her bag, went digging for it because "I need sugar," I said, reeling out a strand. "Especially after that. . . . I guess she likes Seymour better than she thought, huh?"

"*I* like Seymour," Hazel said, a little sharply. "That's all I care about."

"A 72. I've never gotten a 72 in my life. You got—"

"Are you the one?" Keisha said to Hazel, pausing by her seat. "The one who got into the *spirit?*" She sounded fairly pissy herself. Keisha has always been very competitive, not in an evil way, but still. "What'd you get?"

"Who cares?" Hazel said, sharper now. She pulled herself straight, tall and glowering down at Keisha. All her hair was drawn back in a braid, her face was pure sculpture, Lady Vaughn for sure. "It's a fucking English paper, Keisha, who really cares?"

People were logjamming in the doorway now, looking back, Greer and Audrey and "What's the problem here?" Ms. Holzer said, over Greer's shoulder. "Keisha? What's the—"

"Ask *her*," Keisha said rudely and "Fuck off," Hazel shouldering to the door, DJ bag swinging so it almost hit Keisha, Ms. Holzer calling "Hazel!" but she never broke her stride, never looked back at me or anyone, just down the hall and gone—

—and then they all looked at me, Ms. Holzer too, licorice in my hand and "Now I'm going to be *late*," Keisha snapped, really angry so Ms. Holzer scribbled her an excuse, the rest of us dispersing, Audrey and Greer murmuring behind my back so I felt like turning on them, *you fuck off too* but I didn't, I just hurried to Urban Patterns where, although Keisha was late, she got a hundred on her "How

41

to Save a City" animation, and ten points extra credit for the soundtrack; Mr. Khalil loved the soundtrack, it was Leonard Bernstein or Elmer Bernstein or something. I got an 88 on my PowerPoint, "The City Reborn." Afterwards, heading to lunch, Greer said she'd heard that Ms. Holzer was in such a bad mood because her fertility tests had come back negative again.

"Good," Keisha snapped. "The world doesn't need any more people like her."

"Calm down, Keisha," I said. "It's just one grade."

She turned on me then. "I notice your *friend* got a 99."

We stopped in the hallway, facing each other, Greer watching us both with her big blue slightly bugged-out eyes. Greer always reminded me of a goldfish, with those eyes and her frizzy reddish-blond hair floating around her face, like she was perpetually underwater.

"A 98," I said. "So?"

"So," Keisha said, hitching her tote higher on her shoulder, "maybe Ms. Holzer cut her some slack because she's . . ." Keisha stopped.

"Because she's what?"

" 'Diversity,' " she said, making air quotes. "Look it up sometime."

"What's that supposed to mean?" I could feel my heart thumping. I didn't want to argue with Keisha, she was so much faster than I was, and a lot meaner, too. Mean like Julia. But what she was saying, implying—"You're saying she's not smart enough to be here, that she's—"

"I'm *saying* that she comes from a different kind of place than we do. You think her old school, wherever it was, was anything like Vaughn?"

A line in the cafeteria, a lot more brown people, and a much, much lower population of BBGs. A lot more brown people. It suddenly occurred to me, like a jolt, that Keisha was brown. I mean black. African-American. How many African-American Vaughn Virgins were there? African-American BBGs?

"Everyone should be treated the same," Keisha said, arms folded. Greer nodded, in a bobbing cloud of flyaway hair. I didn't say anything, but I thought, We're not the same.

Hazel didn't come to dinner; I hadn't seen her since Lit, and she hadn't answered any of my messages. In the dining hall, the usual table, the usual miso soup and salad and green tea and "These noodles are phenomenally foul," Julia said. She stabbed her chopstick so hard it snapped and flew off somewhere, the ESL girls' table probably but none of them said anything, also as usual. "God, why can't we have some decent food here for a change?"

Audrey was picking apart a rice cake. "What're you so PMS-y for?"

"Shut up, Auds." Julia flicked her gaze at me. "Where were you at lunch? Kells was looking everywhere for you."

"Looking for me where?" I said, and "Down Audrey's

blouse," Alondra said, and laughed. "Just kidding." Audrey laughed, too, a bright little tinkling giggle. I ignored them both and spoke to Julia: "I did homework at lunch. Where did you see Kells?"

"I had to go to Crane—"

"She *snuck into* Crane," someone said, a guy, Patton now magically appearing in his hockey jersey, "snuck into a *boy's room*," leaning down so his lips were next to Julia's ear, but still loud enough for all of us to hear. "Don't tell anybody," he said. "They could expel you, you know."

"It was for the dance," Julia said, suddenly all smiling and kittenish. "I had to get the tally book, didn't I?" and "Hey," in my ear now, Kells, his hands on my shoulders and "Are you done eating?" he said. He had his hockey jersey on, too, he even had his stick and "Dudely," Patton said to him, one arm still around Julia, "did you get a new shaft, man?"

"It's titanium," Kells said, and they both snickered. "My titanium shaft."

"Show it to Mr. Haywood yet?" and they snickered again, Julia laughed too and "What do you want?" I said to Kells. I didn't know if it was just hunger, or what, but I was suddenly in a very bad mood. "I mean, did you want me for something?"

"I want you for everything," he said into my ear, and even though it was supposed to be sexy, or romantic, it sounded like something Patton would say, probably had said and "You're tickling me," I said, too loud and they all looked at me. Patton raised his eyebrows just a little, Kells stood up very straight and "Hey, gentlemen," one of the workers pausing, his hands full of dirty trays. He was as tall as Patton, black hair in a hairnet, blue-and-white uniform speckled with pinkish food stains. "Can I help you all with something?"

Boys weren't supposed to be in our dining room, just like we weren't supposed to be in theirs, *you sure have a lot of asshole rules here* but at the moment I thought it was a good rule, one of the best and "We're fine," I said to the worker guy; I smiled.

"Want to go to practice?" Kells asked me and "I'll walk over with you," Julia said, slipping out of her chair, leaving her tray and plate, broken chopstick and noodle smear. You were supposed to take your things back to the hot station when you were done, but all she did was drop her napkin right in the middle of the mess and walk off with Patton. Kells took a step back and "Lils?" he said, in his own voice, a kind of confused voice so "Just a second," I said, and took my dish back, took some fruit from the fruit bowl, two apricots, cool in the palm of my hand. As soon as we left the dining hall, Kells asked, "All right, what's wrong now?"

Julia and Patton were up ahead, pushing out the main doors towards the practice fields, the sun a yellowish blur behind growing gray clouds. The ice rink was all the way across campus, there was no way I was going to walk that far so I stopped on the path by the flower beds, fleshy little plants with starry pink flowers, the last flowers of the year to bloom. Kells stopped too and "Lils," he said, "what's the matter with you lately?"

"You know, my name is Lily. Why don't you ever call me Lily?"

"I don't know, I— Jesus. OK. Lily, OK? Where've you been?"

"I'm right here."

"I mean before, at lunch. I was looking all over for you—"

Down Audrey's blouse? but it wasn't that, I knew he was kind of a flirt but unlike Patton, Kells, *James*, never really meant it, he never cheated on me so "I went to Lit at lunch," I said. "I have a lot of work due."

"You always say that now. I thought that's why you came to stay on campus, so you'd have more free time, you wouldn't have to, like, drive back and forth—"

"That's not why I came. That doesn't have anything to do—"

"—I thought I'd see you more, but you're always too busy. Or with that Hazel girl, you always have time for *her*."

"Hey dudely," someone passing, Tanner Gustafson, waving his hockey stick. "You coming to practice, or what?"

"In a minute.— Walk over with me? Please?" and for a second he looked like—I don't know, like he used to, like when I first thought I loved him. The way he tipped his head to one side, his wide brown eyes, that scar on his

46

chin, funny little zigzag scar; his mother was always after him to have it lasered off but he always said no: *I like it,* he said. *It's me.* I was there when he got it, falling off the boathouse and splitting his chin open; I was there in the infirmary when the nurse butterfly-stitched the cut together, when they gave him the tetanus shot he squeezed my hand because it hurt, he squeezed my hand now so "All right," I said, "I'll walk with you," down the long path that turned from flower beds to leaf-covered lawn, from gravel to pavement, widening as it got closer to the hockey rink, turning into a little road for cars and service trucks. Patton and Julia had disappeared somewhere up ahead. Had she really sneaked into Crane? That was so monumentally dumb, especially during lunchtime, when anyone could have caught them. She must really want him bad, I thought. Did I want Kells like that? No. Had I ever? No. Not ever like that.

But I *had* wanted him, once. To ask me to dance at the Freshman Fling, big smiling boy in a white shirt and tie, bobbing his head to the music, ambling up to where I stood with Julia and Veronica Chinn and Melissa Marquez; wanted him to be my boyfriend, to message me and send me flowers; to, you know, make love to me, I wanted that, to be with a certain boy, not just to hook up with but someone special, someone you would like to be with. The first time we were together, he smiled, afterwards, a big sleepy smile and I asked him what he was thinking, and he said *I'm not thinking anything; I'm happy.* And he was, really.

He got good grades, he got high, he got me a butterfly charm for my bracelet. A happy person with a happy life.

As we walked, I ate my apricots slowly, so I wouldn't have to talk. At the rink steps we stopped, people, guys, pushing past and around us, sticks and pads and bags and "Lily," Kells said, carefully, "want to come in and watch?" but as if he already knew I didn't, I wouldn't, so when I said "No," he didn't look surprised, just glum, just kissed me and turned away. I tossed the apricot pits in the trash, stuck my hands in my pockets. The clouds had swallowed all the sun now, everything was gray. It was a long walk back to Peacock. I was cold.

When I got to the room, Constance Brill was gone, thankfully. Her bed was humped and lumped with clothes, roll-up skirts and khakis and about a hundred blue crewneck sweaters. Maybe she'd been tidying up, or something. For a change.

I closed the blinds; I clicked on the Japanese light. Ms. Holzer had said at lunch that if I wanted to "amend" my log, she might raise my total grade for the project; she didn't promise, but that was what she implied. But I didn't feel like working on it now, or reading *Franny and Zooey*. What I wanted was to talk to Hazel.

And just as I was reaching for my phone, it rang, and I thought, It's her. But then I saw the number: my mother. If I didn't answer, she'd just keep calling back until I did so

"Hello," as I dragged the comforter up over my feet, blue-and-ivory plaid; Vaughn colors, my mother had picked it out. "Hi, Mom."

"Lily," she said, and paused, took a long breath. "You haven't answered any of my e-mails. Is everything all right?"

"Everything's fine. I answer them, I—"

"Not for the last few days."

"I've been really busy."

"You know, Mrs. Alwin is a little concerned about you."

"Why?" I thought about the 72. "My grades are fine, I'm a 3.75—"

"Grades aren't all there is to school. There's the whole social aspect, too." I knew she was getting at something, heading for something, but as usual she was taking the long way around. The scenic route. She's like that about everything. "One of the things I loved about Vaughn when I was there—and that I appreciate for you, now—is the way you meet so many girls who'll be good friends to you, lifelong friends. Girls who share your background, your values—"

Oh, OK. So this was about Hazel, somehow. What was *wrong* with everybody today? First Keisha, then Kells, now this. "Did Mrs. Alwin call you or something? I know she doesn't like Hazel."

With the name out in the open, my mother's voice changed. "She's concerned, is all. She's said that you two seem to be growing very close these days, and—Lily, Hazel

49

Tobias is new to Vaughn, and she comes from a very different background." Silence, another breath. "Her brother is Duncan Tobias, he's an artist, a photographer—"

Duncan Tobias knows the streets. Is *that* where all those pictures came from? "Is he famous?"

"He's, yes, he's fairly well-known. The point is, they live a very different lifestyle than what you're used to, a very liberal kind of—"

"You mean because of the gayness?"

"*What?* What does— Is Hazel a lesbian, Lily? Is that—"

"No!" although I hadn't even thought about it, I mean I didn't think she was; she didn't have a boyfriend but a lot of girls didn't have boyfriends. And anyway most of the boys were wary of Hazel, except the ones who thought they were hard-core, like Zac Sklar and those guys, but Hazel laughed at them; she told me once *Zachary Sklar wouldn't last five seconds on the street, a lucky sperm boy like that.*

What do you mean, lucky sperm?

You know. Narrowing her eyes even more, she could narrow them literally to slits. *His mommy and daddy have tons of money, but none of it is really his. He didn't earn anything, he was just a lucky sperm. No offense.*

I'm not a lucky sperm, I said. *We don't have lots of money,* because we *didn't* have lots of money, my family, we were just, just normal—

—but my mother was still going on, her voice had gotten louder so "Hazel is not a lesbian," I said. "Her brother is gay. So what? If Mrs. Alwin thinks—"

"It's not that. It has nothing to do with that. The fact is, she's used to a degree of freedom that you simply are not. . . . Your roommate, Constance—why don't you spend more time with her? She's a nice girl, isn't she?"

"She's a total slob. And she's going to fail." Suddenly I felt like laughing, or being mean, or throwing something through the window, I felt like finding Hazel no matter what so "I have to go, Mother," I said, "I have homework," and I closed my phone, turned it to vibrate, clicked off my Japanese light to sit for a minute in the dark, thinking Where would she be?

First I checked her room, then the common room; nothing. Then I thought, She's by the river. I didn't know why I was so sure, but I was, so I went back for my hoodie—black with white lettering, LAMB, from my dad—and slipped out. You were supposed to initial the in-and-out sheet, there was a big sign in Mrs. Alwin's office over the clipboard, WHERE ARE YOU? with a dangling pen, but I didn't. Where am I? Right here, my cold hands in the kangaroo pocket, cutting across the lawn. Bright spots all across the campus, all the dorm room windows, building lights in Admin, security lights shining on the paths between the dorms but I kept to the dark, down the sloping grass to the river path, the evergreen part between Peacock and Crane—

—and right away I saw something under the black trees, bright orange and tiny, a dark shape behind it and "Hazel," I whisper-called, loud enough to carry, so she would know it was me, "Hazel, *hey*," and the orange light snuffed, the dark shape turned into two shapes, two springing bodies as *"Psst,"* from behind me, right behind me, I stopped so fast I almost fell over and "Sheez," Hazel whispered; she was trying not to laugh. "You scared them away. . . . Your friend Julia," nodding. "And General Patton. He was invading her borders. Annexing her tributaries."

"Right there? They were doing it right there?"

"Looked like it. Then he lit up a cigarette, just like in a movie, huh? He probably watches a lot of movies."

"God," I said. "She must be really determined. They just did it at lunch, in Crane."

"Yeah? Super sex machines." Black T-shirt, black men's jacket, she was like a moving shadow, a scarecrow model. "You know, I just came down here to smoke, not watch a porno. . . . What are you doing here?"

Looking for you. "I didn't feel like doing homework," I said. Then I thought, why do I do this, not tell her things, what I'm thinking? What am I afraid of? That she won't like me, that she'll think I'm like Julia and the rest of them, just another lucky sperm? so "Actually," I said, "I was looking for you."

"To not do homework with?"

"To do something with. I don't know."

The breeze was colder here by the water; the leaves

fluttered up by our ankles, swift and dry and "Butterfly ghosts," Hazel said, scuffing at them. "That's what Duncan used to tell me they were. The ghosts of butterflies."

Duncan Tobias. "Is he—he's a photographer, right?"

"Mmm-hmm. Why do you always want to talk about families?"

"Why do you always not?"

She narrowed her eyes at me, even in the dark I could tell. "You start, then."

"All right." And we started walking, back down to the river path, as if we had planned it, as if we had someplace in mind to go. "Um, let's see. I don't have a dog, I never have had a dog. Or brothers and sisters. My father is a lawyer. My mother—my mother just called me, actually, to tell me she was worried about me hanging around with you. But I told her not to, since we weren't hanging around together, since you ran off after Lit and were never seen again, no matter how many times someone tried to find you."

Up ahead the banks got steeper, the river widened, dorms on one side, lawns and trees and the entry building on the other. There was a bridge, fairly new but built to look old, concrete and rounded white river stones, that led to Lady Vaughn with her bow and arrow, and past her to the main road and the highway. If you crossed it, you were technically off campus. You could get in trouble for that, a lot of trouble, if they caught you.

Hazel lit a cigarette. "Your mom is right, I'm a totally

bad influence. Mrs. Whatshername, you know—Franken-stein, the Dean of Girls lady—"

"Mrs. Tai?" She did look a little bit like Frankenstein, she had an extremely long head and very very short black bangs. "She called you into her office?"

"Yup. Her, and Mrs. Dixon, the new-girl lady? And Mrs. Alwin. They sat me down and put a red dot on my file, they said one more offense and I'd have to go before the conduct review board." She kicked at a pebble, an exag-gerated ballet–martial arts kick. "Is that anything like the firing squad?"

"A little. And your parents have to come. . . . Why? What'd you do?" It could have been a lot of things—the smoking for sure, or leaving her room at night, or "mis-conduct," which was one of those all-purpose terms for when a teacher or coach or someone thinks you did some-thing wrong. Like swearing in your Lit class, for instance.

Hazel shrugged. "They think I'm high-risk, or some-thing."

"High risk for what?"

"Just in general."

"Because you're a lesbian?"

"*What?*" She stopped, frowning. "I'm not a lesbian."

"That's what I told my mother," and I started laughing, I couldn't help it, and after a second she did, too, it was all so phenomenally stupid, what were they all so *afraid* of? "High-risk Hazel," I said, still laughing. "The Girl from Somewhere Else."

"It doesn't take much to scare you people, that's for sure, it— Wait, where are you going?"

"Let's cross the bridge," I said. The breeze was higher now, colder, blowing back my hair. My hands were freezing. All of a sudden I felt so good, like if I tried I could fly, just run and leap into the high darkness, into space and "Race you," I said, and started running, really running, as fast as I could which was actually pretty fast, I set a record in lower-school track. She couldn't keep up, I had to wait for her on the other side and "You ought to quit smoking," I said, as she jogged up, coughing.

"Wait a second, I can't breathe. . . . Shit," as we started to walk again, on concrete now, our steps in rhythm. "We better not get caught out here. If I get expelled my brother will have a total meltdown fit."

"Your brother? What about your mom and dad?"

She didn't say anything.

"Hazel?"

She didn't say anything, head down, and then "My parents are dead," she said, loud, much too loud for how quiet it was out there, the cold breeze, the empty road. "I live with my brother, OK? who forced me to come to this fucking place, OK? Is that enough *family* for you?"

She stood staring at me, her eyes wide, so wide, and I stared back at her. Finally "I didn't know," I said. "I'm sorry, I didn't know."

She tipped her head back, back, so she was staring straight up into the air, talking to the air, the darkness. "I said I would come for a year. One year. And I don't really care if I stay or not."

"I care," I said.

It was so unbelievably quiet. We could have been the only people in the world. "Why?" she said. "Why do you even hang around me, Lily? *Lils?* I'm not like your friends, I'm not—"

"*I'm* not like my friends." As soon as I said it, as soon as I heard myself say it, I knew it was true. Even though I had known Julia and Keisha and all of them forever, even though I dressed like them and talked like them and did things like them, somehow I *wasn't* like them; I was like Hazel. And she was like me. It was true.

"Let's go," I said, and started walking again, toward the road, the statue, Lady Vaughn up on the slope and "I'm freezing," Hazel said, but in a more normal voice, falling into step beside me. "What are we doing anyway? Running away?"

"I always thought you looked like her," I said, pointing: the cheekbones, the strong shoulders and "*She* looks like *me*," Hazel said, and we had the same idea, exactly the same idea at exactly the same time. It only took us a few minutes, and when we were done, Lady Vaughn had cigarettes stuck between all of her fingers, all the ones where cigarettes could be wedged anyway, and a Vaughn T-shirt— my T-shirt, but not with my name in it or anything, just a size small which could have been anyone's—tied around her eyes like a blindfold.

"Prepare for the firing squad," I said, shivering in the LAMB hoodie.

"I wish I had a red dot I could stick on her forehead," Hazel said.

"Wait a second," I said, because one of the cigarettes was crooked, I climbed up to straighten it, lost my footing and grabbed for the hand, the fingers—

—and one of them broke, it broke *off*, I couldn't believe it. How could it break? Wasn't she made out of metal, or brass, something indestructible? and Hazel laughed, a loud braying laugh, she slapped her hand over her mouth as I stood there like an idiot, holding this curled piece of cold metal: Lady Vaughn's golden trigger finger, or whatever you call it with a bow and arrow, cracked off at the knuckle.

"Oh my god," I said. Hazel was laughing too hard to talk.

Way out by the road, a flicker of light: headlights, one of the security patrols turning toward campus, toward us and "Run," I said, jamming the finger in my kangaroo pocket, grabbing Hazel's hand, and we ran, gasping, laughing, in the cold and the dark and the feeling of being limitless, boundless, as if we were skimming the ground. All the way back, across the bridge, the evergreen paths, Hazel stifling her coughs as we chugged up and "Wait," I said, at the main Peacock door. "Hide, and I'll buzz," to get whoever was on duty to let me in, so I could sneak downstairs to the laundry, and let Hazel in; she couldn't afford another write-up. But I could. It was my first, actually.

"I was walking by the river," I said, when Mrs. Parais came to the door. "I lost track of the time."

"Well," she said. She looked a little bleary, like maybe she'd fallen asleep. "I'll have to write you up, I'm afraid. . . . I'm sorry, Lily. But rules are rules."

I felt the broken finger in my pocket. "I'm sorry, too," I said, and bit my lip so I wouldn't smile.

I could not believe what an uproar it caused, what we did to Lady Vaughn. You would have thought we spray-painted FUCK YOU in indelible paint across the Admin building. Apparently someone *had* once painted Lady Vaughn, way back in the '70s or '80s or something, gave her black lipstick and nipples: they dug the picture out of the archives and printed it in the *Vaughn Victor*: "That Was No Lady, That Was Vandalism," comparing it to what we did, which was even more ridiculous. It was technically an accident, although to be fair they didn't know that. They also didn't know that the finger was still on campus, stuffed into the back of the gendarme doll sitting on my dresser. I didn't know what else to do with it, I was afraid to just toss it out.

I'd been afraid—not a lot, but a little—about someone putting two and two together, me coming in late (no one knew about Hazel) and the desecration of Lady Vaughn, but Julia, who had come in even later, sneaking in from

Crane—in a huge lapse of judgment, even she admitted that it was—took the attention off me. Of course no one would ever suspect Julia of vandalism, no one on the First Scholar track would ever do anything insane like that. Have sex on the ground, yes, and sneak out to do it, but not break a beloved statue's beloved finger.

We even had an assembly about it: first hour, so Hazel and I weren't sitting together, which was probably good. I ended up between Abby Feldman and Audrey, who both thought it was silly, the whole thing was silly, but "Disparaging your school," said Mrs. Bryce, the Director of Schools, "is disparaging yourselves," as Mrs. Tai stood frowning and nodding behind her. The whole time I kept thinking, *You know, Mrs. Tai really does look like Frankenstein,* and then trying not to laugh. My face muscles were starting to ache.

"Mrs. Bryce is on an opera committee with my dad," Audrey murmured to me. Her breath smelled like mocha coffee. "They're going to Bayreuth again in the summer."

"Beirut?"

"But why do they think it was one of us?" Abby Feldman asked. She was from the south, Alabama or someplace, and everything she said had a question mark at the end of it. "It could have been the town kids?"

"The T-shirt," Audrey said, "obviously," because it was our student-issue shirt, we each got one and only one at the beginning of the year. You couldn't buy them, even the teachers couldn't; they were only for students, each year's slightly different than the last. Now I didn't have one anymore, I'd never have a complete set. Who cares?

"I bet some of the boys did it?" Abby Feldman said.

"God," Audrey sighed, "isn't this over *yet*?" until it finally was and we all shuffled out, the teachers watching for signs of guilt or remorse or something, but no one did anything but grumble and yawn. When I saw Hazel coming up the aisle—tall, serene, wearing her Vaughn student T-shirt for the first time—we didn't laugh, we didn't not-laugh; she just caught my eye, and I caught hers. And that was enough.

Magnus Jespersson

What I've always tried my best to do is honor the boundaries. Duncan and Hazel go back to the beginning together; I'm a much later addition to the family. Really, I only outrank Elbow, and not by that much. . . . That sounds flip, I'm sorry. What I mean is, they have a unique relationship, being brother and sister and, in another way, parent and child. Although they're child and child, too. Losing a parent marks you for life, I think, and both your parents . . . ? Both my parents are living, and I'm an adult. Duncan was just a kid himself when they died, and Hazel was practically a baby.

What I can do, what I try to do, is listen. Just that. I listen to him, I listen to her. In some ways I'm perfectly placed, perfectly balanced, because I understand them both. They are so much alike, you know? Peas in a pod. You would be crazy to try to get between them, and thank God I never have. I mean, there's no space between them, no airspace.

Which is why I was so surprised when Duncan suggested she go to the Vaughn School. She'd been having her woes, jumping from school to school, and friend to friend, looking for the perfect fit. Again, they're so much alike—that was his path, too, going from thing to thing. Until their parents, the accident, you know. That settled him, it had to, he had no choice. It grounded him, but in the best sense, ironically: it gave him a home. He had to make a home for this child, this baby sister, so he did. And in doing that, he made one for himself, too, and me too when I came along. Where Hazel is is our home.

So when she went away to school, actually I wasn't sure what to hope for. For her, I was hoping for a good fit, not just academically—I mean, Hazel is off-the-charts bright, that's not my worry. And she's pretty adaptive—at least, you know, on the surface of things; she knows how to navigate, she knows how to find what she needs, friends, allies, whatever. But I wanted her to find—what she was looking for. Whatever she was looking for. It was kind of surprising to me that she agreed to go—well, "agreed," you know. Because I'd thought she was fairly happy at Bertram High: it's a magnet school, they have a pretty nice mix of kids from all around the city. I was glad when she went there, but Vaughn— Maybe it's a kind of reverse snobbery on my part. But I had my doubts. Hazel is, how can I say this, she's not much for authority, you know? Or "tradition." School colors, and all that Ivy pressure, be first, be the best, it's a lot for a kid to carry around if she doesn't buy into it. At least that's my way of thinking. But hey, I went to Hunter.

What I really believe is, she went to please Duncan. He's the moon and the sun to her, even though she tries not to show it, just like she is to him. So she went kicking and screaming. But she went. . . . Like I said, all I can do, really, is listen. And try to keep an open heart.

5. June

Ms. Nell had left a message in my box, a curled-up yellow MISSED YOU message, so I walked over to the pool. Swim finals were still going on for the freshmen: a semi-fat girl was in the water, kind of panicky and floundering, her cheeks bright red. Ms. Nell squatted by the side of the pool, talking quietly to the girl instead of yelling out directions to her, the way all the other coaches would have, even her assistant, Ms. Bliss. I really liked Ms. Nell; even when she was coaching, she was a teacher first. No, first she was a person, then a teacher, then a coach. It was probably why I did well in the class, better than in field hockey last year, or golf; I had always been a good swimmer, but I swam my hardest for Ms. Nell.

The fat girl got herself back together, a wobbly stroke but at least she was moving again. Ms. Nell looked up and saw me, and smiled, nodding that I should wait on the risers for her, so I did, sitting quiet in the faint chlorine smell, the damp swaddling heat. Once, Julia had written a poem about the natatorium, comparing it to a prenatal state. It was a very good poem actually, about comfort and stillness and floating in the sea inside. I thought that was very descriptive, "the sea inside."

Finally the fat girl hoisted herself out of the water, and another girl got ready to go, a dark girl, narrow and strong-looking, she looked a little bit like Hazel, she looked somehow familiar and "Two minutes, Carla, OK?—Lily, hi. You got my note." Ms. Nell had cut her hair again, soft and feathery-brown around her face; she had a face like a Nordic queen, like the cover of *The Kalevala*, we were doing that next year in World Lit. "Listen, I'm in charge of the sophomore portrait, and I'm way late, Mrs. Parais is really breathing down my neck. Think you could give me a hand with that?"

There were all kinds of goodbye rituals at Vaughn, besides the big one, Convocation. Every year they did a class portrait, you could watch yourself grow up in them if you wanted to, like a flip book. Every class did it a little differently. One year, in lower school, we had to dress as our favorite character in a book. I was Pippi Longstocking, with the braids and everything; it was kind of embarrassingly cute. Julia was Sleeping Beauty, posed in a tiara with her eyes closed. In the boys' picture, Patton was Superman; no surprises there. Kells was Mike, from *Mike Goes to Mars!*, with a little robot bucket-head; I found that sort of endearing. If he did it now, he'd be Superman, too. Super Dudely Hockey Man.

"I'll help," I said to Ms. Nell. "What's your theme going to be?"

"I was thinking of having you all wear your Vaughn shirts."

I started to smile, I couldn't stop myself. "Um, I don't actually have mine anymore," I said.

"Don't have it?"

"I loaned it to a friend, and she—stretched it out."

"Must have been a pretty large friend."

I didn't say anything. They never had discovered who broke off Lady Vaughn's finger; although there had been a few suspects, none of them was ever me. Ms. Nell wasn't exactly smiling, but she didn't look suspicious, and I knew she wouldn't press me about it either way; whatever she might think, she would keep to herself.

"Well, that's too bad," she finally said. "The shirts are all supposed to be keepsakes, of your year, your time here. . . . Have you thought at all about next year, Lily?"

I looked at the water, gleaming pale turquoise under the lights, not harsh fluorescents but individual globes. There was some theory that it cut the glare in the lanes, or something; I didn't care about that, I just loved the way it looked, to float on your back and look up at the lights, and pretend you were swimming in the sky, drifting away into the stars. It reminded me of the night swim, the peace of it, and the loneliness. But the night swim was even better, because then you really were alone. I was alone.

"Lily?"

"I've got your list," I said, because I did, I had it taped inside my planner. Ms. Nell was my adviser, and she had suggested some schools to look at, good suggestions, too, not just total Vaughn clones: Emmsler Academy, and LeMieux in Montreal. Both excellent choices, excellent schools. Vaughn was an excellent school.

"You have the grades to go pretty much anywhere," Ms. Nell said, then "Time, Carla," and the dark girl shot like an arrow into the pool, she was fast, extremely fast. Ms. Nell smiled, at her, then at me.

"She's phenomenal," I said.

"She's my secret weapon next year. . . . Good job, Carla," as the girl climbed out of the pool and walked away, casual, like everyone could do what she did. "You could make the team if you wanted to, Lily. I'd be glad to have you, and the girls would be, too." I didn't say anything. "You know I'm not trying to sway your decision, you have to do what's best for you. But can I ask—you've been at Vaughn all your life. What's changed your mind about it?"

I looked at my feet, the silk flowers on my flip-flops: pink Chanel flowers, my Nana had bought them for me, and a pair for Hazel, too. Matching flip-flops. *Diamonds on the soles of her shoes,* what was that song? Magnus played it on the piano, that song.

"I don't know," I said. "Maybe it's too small for me now."

Ms. Nell didn't say anything. She looked at the water. I looked at the water. The next swimmer stepped up to the line.

Crossing back to the dorm, the slap of my flip-flops on the pavement, the sound of whizzing tires, bike tires and "Lily," someone calling me, a boy, "hey Lily," coming neatly and perfectly to a perfect stop behind me: Edward Flowers, on his canary yellow racing bike. He had a black bandanna tied around his head, like a pirate, he was wearing Hazel's—Duncan's—old green aviator sunglasses. "You coming to dinner with us tonight?"

"Your parents are here?"

"At the airport. They just called." Edward Flowers always looked taller on his bike, like a centaur, a wheeled centaur, though he really wasn't that much taller than I was, both of us at least two inches shorter than Hazel. "They want to go to La Mer. My mom keeps saying it has 'luscious' seafood." And we laughed, because *luscious* was one of our code words, like *urbanity*, or *the finger*; *giving someone the finger* meant playing a trick on them, fooling them in a way they'd never understand, like *I really gave Mr. Brown the finger on that exam.* That one was between Hazel and me only, like *E-flowers* was between her and Edward only, they would say it and crack up. I didn't mind. I wasn't really jealous of Hazel and Edward Flowers, only a tiny bit. But they were right together in a way Kells,

James, and I never were. And Hazel never cut me out of anything, never put Edward Flowers where I should have been. Where I belonged.

"Are you coming?" he asked again.

"Did you talk to B—— Hazel?"

"I called, but," and he shrugged, smiled; Hazel was maddening, that shrug said, but he wasn't maddened, he accepted her not answering the phone, changing her mind, or changing it back; he accepted her. "My parents are coming by at like seven, to Crane. . . . Come if you want to," pivoting the bike like it weighed nothing at all, heading back the way he came, back toward Peacock, and dinner, and Hazel. I kept walking, toward the river, the bridge, the road.

6. December

The amount of food that people donated was phenomenal, which was good and bad. Cans of corn and spring peas and tomato soup, boxes and boxes of cereal and muffin mix, it took the sophomore boys a whole Saturday to sort them all, a fortress of cans piled waist-high beside the folding table where Mrs. Baumgarten, Julia's mother, sat handing out the little needy-family index cards. The cards were marked in a code, like *2A 1C 1Inf* meant two adults, one child, one infant, and each card made suggestions about what that particular family might need, vegetables, baby food, that kind of thing, so you "shopped" through the cans and boxes for that, and packed it all into a box for delivery.

It wasn't difficult, but some people—like a couple of the ESL girls, and Olivia/Oblivia, and Constance Brill—seemed to be having trouble with the concept. Constance especially kept sighing and snuffling and hinting that she could use some help, help from me, but I wouldn't respond; I was avoiding her every chance I got. It was kind of a race, to see if she would leave Vaughn before I had to go to Mrs. Alwin and request a new roommate. She was failing two classes that I knew of, Spanish II and World History of Religion, which was a joke, that was a freshman-level class. A joke, but with Constance, not a surprise.

What I really wanted was Hazel for my roommate. I'd hinted at it from time to time—*I've got to get rid of Constance; whenever you're ready*—but she'd never actually responded. I assumed it was because she didn't want any roommate; having a single was pretty phenomenal. But I never pushed her for an answer. With Hazel, there was always that sense that you could go this far, but no farther, that there were areas that were off-limits: areas in her, and around her. She had let me cross one when she told me about her parents being dead; she let me cross another when she told me that they had died when she was a little tiny girl, like three years old, she could barely remember their faces.

I remember them from pictures, she'd said, one night when we were in the common room eating gorp, she was finishing algebra homework and I was making us little black pleather bracelets, like her infinity bracelet, tight-braided silver and green. *What I see in my mind when I think "Mom" is the picture of her on the piano, the one at the lake, not her in real life, like a real memory. That's so fucking sad, isn't it?*

How old was Duncan then?

Seventeen.

I'd sat there flipping the pleather around and around my finger, thinking *In two years and four months, I'll be seventeen.* What if I had a little sister to suddenly take care of? All by myself? But I'd known enough not to say that, not to say anything, to just keep on braiding and eating gorp. Hazel was like a wild creature sometimes, you had to let her come to you, especially when she was upset. She could let you get close and then take a chunk out of you; she'd done it to me a couple of times before. But it was never personal, I mean it always seemed to have more to do with her, her internal weather, than with me. A lot of Hazel had to do with just Hazel. And she wasn't ever abusive, or nasty, like Keisha could sometimes be, or Julia.

Julia in fact had been fairly abusive throughout this whole canned food drive, arguing against dropping off the food ourselves, *I don't have time to go all the way to some shelter.* And cutting her eyes at Tara Bream, who was one of the Wilmingtons, the free-ride scholarship students: *Maybe Tara knows some other people who could use our help. Maybe Tara could lead a clothing drive.*

Audrey's theory for Julia's nastiness, as loyal second-in-command, was that Julia was student chair of the drive and Mrs. Baumgarten was parent chair, and Julia and her mother obviously couldn't stand each other, although "I don't know why," Audrey said. She had a giant can of pears in each hand, she looked like she was doing curls. "They're so much alike, they're practically the same person."

"That's why," Keisha said, ripping tape. "Two Baums in

one Garten. This town ain't big enough for the both of us, sheriff."

I thought Keisha was probably right, but I didn't say it to her; I didn't say too much to her anymore. Ever since the Lit class incident, she and I hadn't really been friends, because I thought she'd way overreacted, and said so; and even more, because I was so close with Hazel now. Keisha and I weren't enemies, but we'd stopped walking to Urban Patterns together, and we never sat next to each other in the dining hall—when I ate in the dining hall, which wasn't all that often. Hazel and I mostly took our food somewhere else, to an empty classroom or lecture room, or down by the river if it was a sunny day. Technically you weren't allowed to do that, but people did it all the time: you said you had homework, or a class project, or a sports thing you had to be at, and the dining hall monitors would let you go. They knew you were lying, they didn't care.

The dining hall workers didn't care either, like Mrs. Beebe, who joked with us about our excessive café crème consumption, or Alonzo, who I teased Hazel was crushing on her; he was, too. He was older, like twenty maybe, and kind of cute, in a shaggy way. He always made sure to linger by the kitchen doors to give her a smile or a wave, waiting for her to glance his way before he said anything. . . . It's funny, I never really noticed Alonzo, or Mrs. Beebe, until Hazel came.

Hazel had made lots of little changes like that for me, as if her being at Vaughn was a kind of window, or camera, showing me parts of it that I'd never seen before; she opened my eyes. And Vaughn had changed her in some ways, too. She'd stopped talking so much about how tough Bertram High was, stopped holding herself so apart from the little ultra-Vaughn rituals, like going to Sunday brunch, or the every-other-Friday movie nights. Once I saw her on the Admin steps, writing something in a notebook; at first she wouldn't show me, but finally *It's nothing*, she said, *just a sketch,* actually a pretty excellent sketch of the building's façade, the stone baskets of roses and apples and *It's a cool building,* she said, slightly defensive. *Cool to draw, that's all.*

I like the natatorium better.

No, that's way too industrial. And then she told me about all of the old things at Vaughn, the interesting things she'd noticed, that I must have stopped seeing a long time ago: the way the carpets in the upper school library were kind of falling apart *like old velvet,* she said, *when it's rubbed so soft it's worn through. Or the way it is when you're sitting in the little part of the church, the chapel? Is that what it's called, where they have the singing?* That was something new, too, that she would sometimes ask questions, instead of acting as if she already knew the answer, or didn't care anyway. *It's like an old castle or something in there. Medieval . . . I like the medieval-ness, that's one of the pluses here. The few pluses.*

Besides the café crèmes, right? And the flowers.

She laughed a little; she knew I meant Edward Flowers. He'd followed her all around at the Halloween dance, like it was finally time to make his move: first asking questions about our costume—we were the Bash Sisters, I was Clash Bash and she was Slash Bash, from this really obscure anime series she'd gotten me into: black T-shirts, black wristbands we made out of electrical tape, black paint-stick in long smears around our eyes—and then just talking, joking with her in his calm dry way that wasn't like joking at all, not like so many of the other boys did; their jokes were mostly about showing you how funny they were, not about making you laugh. Edward Flowers made Hazel laugh, really laugh, once or twice. It was one of the pluses about that dance, the few pluses.

The benefit part was fine, they raised a lot of money for New Horizons. Patton got center stage for the announcement, in his hockey jersey "costume": *The work that went into this, god, you guys would never believe it.* As if he'd done the whole event single-handedly. Beside him onstage, Keisha raised her eyebrows. Edward Flowers smiled and didn't say anything.

The New Horizons ladies were so nice, it was sort of embarrassing. They stood by the punch table in their costumes—deely-bobbers and a sparkly top hat—and kept smiling and thanking everybody who passed by; they thanked me twice, and I hadn't done anything.

Two New Horizons girls came, too. At first I thought they were in costume, but really they had just dressed like—like themselves: one in a way-too-tight green velveteen minidress, one in a low-cut stretch top, white jeans, and a baseball cap. Both of them were pregnant. The minidress girl was *huge*.

And they were loud, really loud, and silly, dancing with each other, stuffing their purses full of Halloween candy from the bowls. No one really wanted to talk to them, although some people tried, mostly when the teachers were watching, like Julia, who acted all friendly for two minutes, then never looked at them again for the rest of the night. She made a point of telling Mrs. Bryce *I'm so glad we were able to do this,* looking all earnest and kindly. *These girls can really use our help.*

It's all so patronizing, Hazel said to me, narrowed paintstick eyes, loud enough for Julia to hear. *<u>Ma</u>tronizing.*

And Julia thinned out her lips, exactly the way her mother did, and said *I don't agree, I think it's nice to help people who need it.* And suddenly I felt ferociously annoyed and said *No one from First Scholar is here, Julia, OK?*

What's that supposed to mean?

I'm going to go dance with them, Hazel said, and did: in the middle of the dance floor, the girls shouting out the words to the song, and laughing, Hazel started laughing, too. She seemed—I don't know, freer—no, that wasn't the word, I didn't know what the word was. And I didn't know why watching her made me so . . . uncomfortable. But it did. Which made me uncomfortable in a different way, at myself, as if I were—ashamed of myself, or something. That Hazel could like those girls in a way that I couldn't, or didn't want to; would never want to. That I wished she wouldn't dance with them, laugh with them. That I wished they were gone, or had never come in the first place, with their thick pink lipstick and their too-tight clothes and their obviously pregnant stomachs, like refugees from a place you wouldn't want to go. I was glad when the song ended, when the dance was done.

But when I got my index card from Mrs. Baumgarten, I remembered those girls: *1A 1C,* that could have been one of them. One adult in a baseball cap, one child grabbing at the low-cut top. Then I thought, It could have been Duncan and Hazel, too. One semi-adult seventeen-year-old, one three-year-old child, both of them orphans. Did they ever have to do something like New Horizons? Social services, or whatever that's called? Charity handouts, bags of canned food that someone else chose for you.

Thinking that, seeing it, made me a better shopper, pickier: I made sure to take the organic apple juice, the baby cereal with enriched vitamins, the box of protein bars because if you were someone like Duncan, say, trying to go to school or whatever, you wouldn't have a lot of time to make meals for yourself, maybe you wouldn't have any time at all after taking care of your little sister. So you'd have to eat something on the run, and protein bars were good for that. Also the microwave burritos, they were easy. And those cheese-and-cracker things—

"What's taking you so long?" Greer Reinhardt asked me. Her shopping bag was filled with stupid things:

canned asparagus, milk substitute, a coupon for bagels and "That stuff doesn't even go together," I said.

"What?" She squinted at her index card. "It says vegetable, dairy, bread."

"It's not a math problem, it's a menu. For people to eat. Would you eat it?" Greer gave me a weird look and walked away. Hazel breezed past with her shopping bag: canned corn, minestrone soup; I saw she'd picked the organic juice, too.

"This is incredibly boring," she said. "I'm glad Magnus does all the grocery shopping at home."

"How can you say that? Maybe Edward Flowers stacked those very cans. With his very own hands. . . . He's seriously crushing on you, in case you didn't notice. It's kind of too bad you're a lesbian."

She smiled. She smiled a lot, when I talked about Edward Flowers. "Yeah, kind of."

Julia heard us, overheard us, and smiled, too, her I'm-just-kidding smile which meant of course the opposite: "Well, Edward Flowers is kind of gay, anyway, so you two are sort of perfect for each other. . . . Just kidding."

Hazel and I didn't say anything, just glanced at her, at each other. Alondra heard her and frowned. "Why do you say that? I mean, I don't care if he is or isn't, I don't care who's gay. But—"

"Well, Edward Flowers is in Glee Club, and tennis—"

"Oh Julia, come on. That's such a stereotype."

"Well OK, it can be. I agree. But take someone like

Patton, he's the captain of the hockey team, *and* the lacrosse team, and he's—"

"Sporty guys," Audrey said, "are always studly." I knew she was thinking of Kells, knew it more when she glanced at me—I don't think she was even aware she was doing it: *Kells = Kells' girlfriend.* Soon to be ex-girlfriend; but she didn't know that. Kells didn't know it, either. Sometimes even I didn't know it. Like last Friday, he'd gone to movie night with Hazel and me: they were showing this old thriller from the '80s, with the insane hair and the shoulder-pad suits, and Kells kept laughing at Hazel's remarks, trying to ping-pong back with some of his own, even though hers were a thousand times faster and funnier, and we all knew it, even Kells. Afterwards, walking back, Hazel said to me, *You know, ESPN Boy is occasionally OK.*

I know, I'd said back. And I did know. He kind of liked Hazel, too, which I hadn't ever expected, he said she was "off-center," but in a good way. But he still didn't understand why we were friends, he still thought that she was changing me, taking up too much of my time, time I could have spent with him. But I didn't want to, Hazel or no Hazel I wouldn't have gone to Crane to watch basketball games on their room-size TV, or to the restaurant one of the day students' parents owned, where they sneaked beer in the back, and smoked all the way home. And Kells and I still did things together, we still hooked up sometimes. But sometimes was only—sometimes. And afterwards I always felt tired. . . . Actually Edward Flowers was a lot more fun to hang with, and he wasn't even interested in me, not that way.

They're always telling you that in the magazines, you know, that a boy should be your friend first, before you ever think of hooking up with him. But that wasn't my experience with Kells, or Benjamin Partridge, who was my first boyfriend really, back in eighth grade, the first boy I ever let do things to me, the first boy I ever wanted to do more than kiss. I didn't have a ton of boyfriends, I wasn't in a huge hurry like Alondra, who went through boys like snacks, one bite and she was done, or Sandra Dumars, who wasn't at Vaughn anymore, she'd been expelled for plagiarism although they could easily have expelled her for sex: she was hooking up with half the freshman boys at the same time. Hazel had had a lot of boyfriends, a string of names she ticked off on her fingers as we walked back to Peacock from the movie—

Well, there was Justin Wymer—this is like ninth grade and up, right, middle school doesn't count—and Bobby Bloom, you would have liked him, he was funny. He could really dance, too. Cas Elezar, his mom was the nurse at Alice Ungers—

What's Alice Ungers?

A school I went to. Briefly. We used to steal condoms from her office. But Cas was a little bit too much of an alcoholic for me. Then Mikel, he was hot, *he was gorgeous. No one could figure out what he was doing with me. . . . He was a huge freak, though,*

79

he kept wanting me to try things, sex things she wasn't ready for, she didn't know what else to do but break up with him but *You could have just said no,* I said. *That's what I do with Kells.*

ESPN Boy likes to go icky?

I wouldn't call it icky, but he'd like to do stuff I don't want to.

What kind of stuff? so I told her, walking in the darkness, the chill seeping in through the LAMB hoodie, making me shiver. Hazel wore a wool coat, a man's peacoat, Duncan's old peacoat. No one else was around, just the two of us in the cold.

But really, I said, *he really just wants the normal stuff. All the time.*

Edward Flowers, Hazel said, *hasn't even tried to kiss me yet.*

He kisses you with his eyes, I said, because it was true.

Now Hazel looked at Julia from her full height, shopping bag at her feet, arms folded and "You know something?" she said. "I know a lot of guys like Patton Ponder. My old school was full of them."

"Really?" Julia said. "No offense, Hazel, but I sort of doubt that."

"I don't mean rich guys," Hazel said. "I mean guys who'll fuck anything that holds still for it. No offense, Julia, but they're everywhere. Once you get out into the real world, you'll see." Alondra laughed. Hazel walked away with her shopping bag. Julia made a face at Audrey, who made the same face back. I smiled at them both, then went back to my shopping, to find some chicken noodle soup for 1C. Little kids always like chicken noodle soup.

Hazel was on her bed, sticking dark blue fabric tape to a dark blue T-shirt, IT'S THEM OR US but she was turning it into S M U and "Voilà," she said. The room smelled like tuberose air freshener, Cherry Hot licorice, and, very very faintly, cigarettes. "*Now* it's a college: Southern Methodist University. Or Sado-Masochistic U. Whichever."

"Or—" I couldn't think of anything funny. "Aren't you going to dinner?"

"I already ate."

"What, the rest of the licorice?" as her phone rang, a complicated little trill, a song I didn't know and "Hey," she said, "hey, hi," and then looked at me, the look that means *I need some privacy* so "I'll see you later," I said, although I wanted to stay, why couldn't I stay? Who was she talking to, that she didn't want me to hear?

Back in the hallway I saw she had a new picture taped to the door, a hard-hat guy staring down a manhole, as if you were in the manhole staring up. Or in. I stared at him, feeling more and more—what's the word?—disgruntled. Completely disgruntled. Behind the door I could hear Hazel: no words, just the murmur of her voice.

A part of me, a tiny part, wanted to stand there and listen, but I would never do that. So I headed for the dining hall, it was dinnertime anyway. In Peacock most of the rooms were empty, but a few people were doing home-work, or going to practice: two girls with violin cases, an-other with a tennis racket.

Down the hall, down the stairs, look out for the chipped slate on the third step from the bottom, don't snag your jacket on the railing's metal lip. Out the door, cross the path, scatter of gravel, I could find my way to the dining hall with my eyes closed, I could find my way any-where on campus blindfolded in the dark. That's what happens when you've been somewhere for almost eleven years. Eleven *years*. Was this all I was ever going to know? The buildings, the trees, the way the brown grass sloped down to the river that ran cold and sluggish now, dead leaves, broken sticks; when January came it would freeze everywhere but the center, the deepest water still in mo-tion, even in the heart of the ice. January, when we came back from winter break.

I'd talked to Hazel about break, a little, but she hadn't said much, just that she was going home, which I already knew. But like everything to do with home, with Duncan and Magnus, there was that sense of a line that I couldn't cross; it was really starting to bother me. I didn't want to—invade her, I just— If you're someone's friend, best friend, don't you let her in? She didn't want to be my roommate, she didn't want to tell me about her plans—I'd tell her about *my* plans, even though I didn't have any—my family had plans, my mother, she always made such a huge deal out of the holidays. A bunch of people were going ski-ing, I'd been invited to that, and Julia's family was doing their usual New Year's thing. Last year I'd gone just for the weekend. She wouldn't invite me this year, though, which would save me the trouble of making up an excuse not to go. Even if we were still good friends, which we weren't, going to Julia's would be like staying at Vaughn. *Everything* was like staying at Vaughn: going home for break, going to the dining hall, sitting at my old table in my old stupid seat—

—where I immediately got into a stupid argument with Devi Gupta about grade inflation. She was sticking up for Mr. Haywood, who was known as a total jock slut: boy or girl didn't matter, any jock in his class got at least a B for standing up straight but "You're being unfair," Devi said, shredding her straw paper with her blunt red fingernails. "He just respects the extra effort you have to go through if you're in sports."

"All of us are 'in sports,' Devi, we all play some kind of—"

"I mean *committed* to sports." Devi was the queen of girls' basketball. "Mr. Haywood understands the extra—"

"Mr. Haywood wants to win, period. He doesn't care about anything else." Was that my voice? I sounded so—fierce, fierce and irritable, everyone at the table was look-ing at me now—

—and "Hey," Hazel said. Somehow she had appeared

behind me, holding an empty plate. "I can hear you yelling all the way from the hallway," she said. "Your blood sugar must be low."

"My blood sugar is fine. And I'm not yelling," but I followed her to the hot station, where she made me a personal pizza: lots of veggies, lots of hot peppers and "Are you trying to kill me?" I said. I still sounded intensely irritable. "There are easier ways."

"No, I'm trying to, what's the word?" She sprinkled on some slightly stinky cheese, goat cheese. "Acclimate you?"

"Acclimate me to what?"

She smiled, a wide and satisfied smile, popped a pepper in her mouth: "To my house," she said, chewing. "You're coming home with me for winter break."

"Well," my mother said, after a breathy pause, "that would be nice. Some other time. But not this Christmas, sweetie. We're all meeting at Sea Springs, Nana and Papa and Aunt Elizabeth—"

"I don't want to go to Sea Springs," I said, fishing one-handed under my bed for my Blondy boots, where were they? Hazel had said to bring shoes I could walk in, she was going to show me all the neighborhood. Her neighborhood. And Magnus was going to take us shopping, and to the Octagon Gardens, and to the dog park with Elbow; he said I'd love the dog park. He said he was looking forward to meeting me: *Any friend of Hazel's, you know, but especially any friend with a jones for Cherry Hot. Do you know they now make it in blueberry, too? It's called Blueberry Ice.* He had a slow, calm, slightly accented voice, a voice that you could listen to just for the music of it, just for the sound—

—unlike, say, my mother's voice, getting sharper and sharper as I kept on saying no: no to Sea Springs, no to turkey dinner after midnight church, no to going home, period, because I was going to Hazel's no matter what but "Why are you being so obstinate, Lily? This just isn't like you."

That made me smile. I tried to keep it out of my voice. "I've done Christmas your way for my whole life, Mother." I found one boot, chunky black heel, hauled it out; I found the other. "I want to do things my way for once."

"You went to the Baumgartens' for New Year's last year."

"So why can't I go to Hazel's for Christmas this year?"

"What about James? I was going to ask you to invite him, too."

I had to think for a minute: who is James? Then "Oh," I said. We hadn't actually fought about what to do over break, because "He's going to Patton Ponder's," I said. "And then his dad's taking them skiing." I didn't ski, and Kells knew that. He'd still wanted me to come, though, and was pissed that I wouldn't. That I had somewhere I wanted to go more. Much more.

"Your father won't be at all happy about this, you know. First you want to stay on campus, and now—"

"He doesn't even care about the holidays. You're the one who cares." She didn't say anything, just that pause, that breath. That intake breath. . . . "Mother? *Mother*, are you *smoking?*"

"What?" A different kind of pause. "Lily, don't try to change the—"

"You are! You're smoking again," because I had suddenly recognized those little sounds, those pauses: not breaths but puffs, puffs on a cigarette, my dad would be so furious if he knew. She had gone through a program, two programs, she had had an addictions coach and everything. "You promised you would stop, you said—"

"That's not the issue here. The issue is—"

"Does Dad know?"

Silence. I could picture her smoking furtively in her car, the windows rolled down so the smell wouldn't get into her clothes, or huddled out on the deck, in the cold, the way Hazel did. "He'd be angrier about that than about me not coming home," I said, calm now because I knew I'd won, I knew she wouldn't try to stop me so "Mother," I said, "it's not that I don't want to see you, and Nana and Papa and everybody. I just—I need my own life, you know."

She didn't say anything for a minute, a fairly long minute, no more cigarette sounds and then "Your father will call you later," she said. "Goodbye." And hung up.

He didn't call me. Mrs. Alwin did, into her office.

"And she said, 'You've always been a stellar student, Lily,' "
slurring *stellarstudent*, all one word, looking over my imagi-
nary glasses. Hazel was grinning. Magnus was gathering
plates. " 'But you've changed since you met Hazel Tobias.
And we are *allconcerned*.' "

"That's amazing," Magnus said; he winked at Hazel. "I
didn't realize you were quite so controversial, baby girl."

"I'm not," Hazel said. "It's just that *Lils* is so terribly
fucking special. She's the ultimate lifer, behind her back
everyone calls her Lady Vaughn."

"Shut up," I said. "Don't make me break off your finger."

She laughed, pushed her plate aside, empty plate with
dregs of rice and curry; Magnus had made an amazing
curry casserole thing, with cucumber-yogurt sauce to cut
the heat. I hadn't used any sauce, I loved it hot. I loved
that Hazel smoked at the table, and swore when she felt
like it, I loved that Magnus had had cappuccino waiting
when we came in, that he hugged me right after we shook
hands, that Elbow wiggled so hard for Hazel that he fell
over on his fat little back. Everything that had happened
so far, I loved.

And I loved their apartment, the way one thing leaned

up against another: the wavy green window glass in the bathroom, framed by wax-paper ivy; the bright cartoon bedsheets (Super Kitty, in the guest room where I was) and a super-soft ivory Porthault quilt; the statues of naked Greek gods and Holy Marys and Beethovens or whoever, all the little glass and plaster people standing around on the sideboard watching you eat. Some looked old, very old, antique; one still had its sticker from a dollar-discount store. All these things that couldn't belong together, but somehow they did.

"So," Magnus said, clearing plates. "The upshot with Miss Hannigan was—?"

"Well . . . I'm staying until December 30," I said after a pause, thinking *Who's Miss Hannigan?* "Then I have to go meet my parents at Sea Springs."

"Sea Springs, wow. That's not much of a punishment." Magnus smiled. He had a quick smile, but not a fake one, he was just—pleased. By Sea Springs, by the way the curry turned out; by Hazel especially, he had a special smile for her, I could see that. *Baby girl.* He liked giving nicknames, I could see that, too. He called Elbow "Macaroni" and "Tennis" and something else that sounded Swedish-y, *hund.*

And when the deadbolt turned "Ah," he said, with another special smile, tossing down the potholder, "the melancholy Dane," as Duncan came in, late and gloomy, Duncan who looked so much like Hazel I had to do a double take, him to her to him again, triple take: the same

long face, the same eyebrows, the same narrowed No Tres-
passing look as "This is Lily Noble," Magnus said, his hand
on my shoulder and "I know that," Duncan back, sharp,
then formally to me "Good to meet you," long fingers like
Hazel's, strong and cold. "I'm Duncan Tobias."

"I know that," I said, a joke, but it didn't come out
funny and he didn't smile, turned his stare and "Bone, a
minute?" as Hazel slipped out of the chair, followed him
down the hall, into another room and "We live a fairly her-
metic life," Magnus said, as voices came from behind the
door, Hazel's getting louder: "—up to me, it's my vacation,
isn't it?"

"Everything in this house isn't all about you."

"And, to be honest," Magnus said, "he was looking forward to some alone time with his sister. She's never been
away this long before."

"I understand," I said. I could feel my face turning
pink, but a part of me was—I don't know—glad, glad that
Magnus had just told me what was what, no evasion, no
fake politeness. Because I *had* kind of disrupted their to-
getherness, even though "She invited me," I said, then immediately hated the way it came out, like a little kid so "I
mean," I said, red, "I don't want to be a problem for anybody."

Magnus paused, scraped plate in hand, Elbow at his
feet, and "Lily," he said, "you cannot be a problem." And
the way he said it—simply, like it was the most obvious

truth in the world, Lily Noble cannot be a problem. . . .
"Grab those water glasses, yes?" Magnus said, and I did.

Everywhere I had ever been, I never had to think about
the right way to act: I just knew. Because it was always the
same, it was like a game I knew how to play, was born
knowing. But at Hazel's it was different. And I was different, too. . . . No, I wasn't. I was just—more. More of myself. That's what was different.

We did all the things Hazel had said we would. We went
to the Octagon Gardens, two-story steamy greenhouse
windows, knobby cactus and trailing bougainvillea, the
scent of the climbing roses like little airborne bursts of
spice. In the gift shop, I bought some sugar made from
those same spicy roses, and Magnus put it in a sauce. We
went shopping—God, did we shop, all these little hole-in-
the-wall boutiques, hand-stenciled blouses and dangly
jade earrings and palm-size purse mirrors trimmed in fake
pony fur, I bought a dozen just of those, to give away.
Hazel took me on a walking tour of her neighborhood, the
cafés and bodegas, the pocket park on the corner where
people hung out to smoke and kiss, guys in parkas and
thug caps, girls with smudgy eyeliner and skin-tight Jessicka jeans and "That used to be me," Hazel said, hands
jammed in her peacoat pockets, her voice half muffled by
her scarf. Magnus had given us scarves to wear, a spare
one of Duncan's for her, his for me, long and blue and

cashmere-blend. "I spent so much time here, you wouldn't believe. This is where I met Bobby Bloom, 'member I told you about him?"

"I remember."

We went uptown, to the Sweetheart Shop, *they have all kinds of weird candy there*: not only Cherry Hot and Blueberry Ice but things like marzipan, and chocolate-covered ants, and bright blue packets of tiny sugar skulls. Magnus told us about being in Mexico for the Day of the Dead, how people ate the skulls at cemetery picnics, and made little altars, *ofrendas*, and how the monarch butterflies came south right about that time "like the spirits of the dead," Magnus said, unwrapping a jalapeño chocolate. "Coming home to roost."

"Butterfly ghosts," I said to Hazel. "Remember? The leaves?" They both looked at me; Hazel nodded. And then Magnus looked at Hazel, his head to one side.

Everywhere we went was decorated for the holidays, the blue-and-silver of Hanukkah, the red-and-green of Christmas, even at the dog park there was a wreath on the gate, right above the PICK UP AFTER YOUR POOCH! sign. Magnus was right, I did love the dog park: dachshunds and Jack Russells and every kind of mutt, the people standing together like parents at a playground, bundled up and chatting, making sure the dogs didn't get too rough. Hazel was very protective of Elbow, overprotective, Magnus said: "He's a dog, baby girl. He can take care of himself."

"He's old and fat," Hazel said, glaring at a golden retriever who had knocked Elbow down: she looked like she wanted to bite the dog herself, eyes narrowed to slits, arms crossed; she looked exactly like Duncan then.

I hardly ever saw Duncan, he was almost never home. But in a way he was always there, in his pictures all over the walls, faces from everywhere and "Where was this taken?" I asked Magnus, about a picture of a tall thin black man with dyed-blond hair, huge white-framed sunglasses, he looked phenomenally exotic but "Actually," Magnus said, "I believe that was just a few blocks from here. Now this one, this was from a fashion job in Morocco," a girl not much older than me or Hazel, actually she looked kind of like Hazel, the same kind of long strong face, I said so and "Oh yeah," Magnus agreed, "a real Modigliani," what did that mean? Afterwards I looked it up (Amedeo Modigliani, a painter, all his people had those kinds of faces), like I looked up Miss Hannigan, and Seymour; they seemed to know so much more than I did, Magnus and Hazel. About everything. I think I loved that most of all.

The day before Christmas Eve, gray afternoon and snowing, a wet miserable snow no fun to walk in, so Hazel was online, and I was browsing in the hallway like it was an art gallery, it *was* an art gallery. Standing there squinting at a picture of a couple wrapped up in robes or blankets, kissing in an alley made of stone and "That's Montmarte,"

Duncan said, from right behind me; I jumped, I couldn't help it. "In Paris."

"I've been to Paris," I said, why did I say that? even though it was true, but I'd only been there twice, once when I was like six years old or something, my mother bought me the gendarme doll there.

Duncan didn't answer. *Duncan Tobias knows the streets.* I wanted to talk to him; I was a little afraid of him; I didn't really know what to say. Finally "Hazel's got a lot of your pictures," I said into the silence, his silence. "At school, I mean. They're all over her room."

"Really," he said, eyebrows up, he walked away then but he mentioned it again at dinner: "I hear you have my stuff in your room," which made Hazel instantly glare at me, why? and Magnus sighed, and Elbow hid under the table when the yelling started, it got louder and louder—

"I *take* all those jobs for you, Bone, to keep you in school. Do you think I want to shoot every stupid fucking model in the—"

"Don't do it, then, I don't want you to do it, I didn't even want to go there in the first place. You're the one who—"

"If Mom and Pop were—"

"Don't start." Hazel sounded meaner than I'd ever heard her; if I didn't know her I would have been scared. I *was* a little scared. "I'm done with all that, I'm not going to let ghosts run my life."

"Don't say that. Don't ever say that. You didn't know them, you don't know what they wanted for you—"

"It's not my fault I didn't know them! 'Mom and Pop, Mom and Pop,' I'm so fucking *sick* of—"

—and Magnus drew me into the little pantry then, had me grind the beans for coffee as "Don't let it bother you," he said, but he looked sad. "They'll get over it. They always do. Two peas in a pod, really."

"They sound like they're going to—start hitting, or something."

"I don't exist to make you happy, Duncan!"

"Good! You don't!"

The pantry door nudged open: Elbow, trembling. Magnus picked him up for a cuddle, then slipped the leash from the rack. "It's stopped snowing," he said to me. "Let's take him for a walk."

The yellowy streetlights made the gray slush darker, our breath hung in the cold damp air. Elbow insisted on stopping for every newspaper box and trash can, sniffing and considering, and Magnus talked: about the places we passed—this place had great goat cheese, that place was totally overpriced—and then about Duncan. How hard he tried, how worried he was when Hazel went through what Magnus called her "blue period," jumping from school to school, boyfriend to boyfriend, making friends then dropping them and "It's been difficult," Magnus said. He wore Duncan's scarf, too long for him, bunched up at his chin. "He's tried to do his best for her. But he was so young, when . . ." His voice trailed off. I thought of the parents, *Mom and Pop*; I'd seen the picture on the piano, a dark-haired lady waving in a bathing suit, her eyes squinted against the sun: Hazel's mother. Duncan's mother. "And he's not really the father type."

"Neither is my father," I said. Elbow paused to sniff a crushed-up takeout bag. "I mean, I know it's not the same, but— He doesn't know what to do, with me, I mean. Especially when I won't do what he wants." *Why would you want to leave Vaughn, Lily? What's the problem?* "At least Hazel and Duncan can fight together."

"What's your dad like?"

"He's a lawyer," I said, and then realized how sad that was, that that was the first thing I thought about him, the only thing I thought to say; so "What do you do?" I asked, to kind of change the subject. "I mean, like a job, or something."

"Well," Magnus said, tugging the bag away from Elbow, who was chewing it in a fast gulpy kind of way, one eye up to check if we were watching, "my official title is audio architect, but what I am is basically a DJ," at Music to Your Ears, the purple-and-white swag was all around the apartment, coffee mugs and pens and "What we do," steering Elbow around a pile of unknown poop, "is use music to enhance an experience," matching songs to songs for restaurants and stores, Rocket System with the Beatles with Tica Coover with jazz with whatever. He told me about different places requesting different kinds of soundtracks, not just clothes stores needing to sound cool, but like a florist wanting music from every place in the world that roses grow, and a chain of toy stores wanting music like cartoons "but not *from* cartoons," Magnus said. "No Looney Tunes, no 'Alice in the Palace,' nothing like that. It was a challenge, I'll tell you. But I managed to pull together a program."

"You like your job?"

He winked. "I'd do it for free. Just don't tell my boss."

And I thought how strange that was, not just that there was such a job (although I'd never heard of it before, I'd never even considered how music got into stores and things, I assumed it just—occurred somehow), but that you could do something without really thinking of the money, because your job was fun. I couldn't imagine my dad having fun at work. *I take all those jobs for you, Bone, to keep you in school.* Is that how my dad felt, too?

"Why does Duncan call her Bone?" I asked.

"It's a family nickname," Magnus said, after a minute. "A pet name. Don't your parents have one for you?"

I shook my head. My mother occasionally called me "sweetie" but that didn't count, that was anonymous. I told him about "Kells" and "Lils," then about Julia and Alondra, and how being friends with Hazel was so different. "It's not just that I've known them all my life," I said. "It's that *she's* different, she's—"

"You rhyme," Magnus said. "You two."

We walked the rest of the block in silence, what he'd

said ringing in my head like a bell, *you rhyme*. So he could see it, too. At the door, scraping our shoes and "You should have worn a hat," Magnus scolded. "Your hair's so wet, it's practically black. . . . I bet your hair was white as a baby."

"It was. It was like dandelion fluff. I hated it."

"No, not a dandelion, a lily—a calla lily. Do you know how rare your coloring is, that porcelain blond? The boys must run after you like fallow deer."

And I smiled, pleased, confused: fellow deer? Another thing to look up. *Porcelain blond*, that sounded so beautiful.

Inside it was quiet, just the faint hum of TV. I peeked in Hazel's room: she was on her bed, smoking and "Where'd you guys go?" she said. She didn't sound mad anymore, just tired.

"Out to walk Elbow." I perched on the edge of the bed, Elbow hopped right up and "Get your wet-ass paws off me," Hazel said, hugging him. "What've you been eating, piggy?— Hey," to me. "Guess what?"

"You're quitting smoking?"

"No. We're going to a party tomorrow at a club, some of—some people I know from Bertram." She put out her cigarette. She had been crying, I could tell. "It'll be fun," she said.

The club was called Braid, the drinks were phenomenally awful—I had a Passionflower, passion fruit vodka and

97

lime juice, it tasted like alcohol shampoo—and the girls, Hazel's Bertram friends—still her friends?—didn't like me at all.

At first I thought they did. They all crowded around me in their black pants and blue eyeliner, and asked a lot of questions: about school, and where I came from, and was I having fun in the city so far? They complimented my long hair—theirs was all cut short—my Mahalo jeans, my Tiffany charms—"Ooh, look, a butterfly"—and smiled at each other, at Hazel who wasn't smiling at all. Then the main girl, Dia, said, "It's *so* precious. Just like something my mom would wear."

My face turned pink, I didn't say anything, I didn't know what to say. Hazel said, "Don't be such a bitch, Dia."

From then on they all totally ignored me and talked to each other, to Hazel, about stuff I didn't know, names and places, things that happened—*they went wild at Fisher's party, oh Koki's such a freak*—as I sipped my sour drink, as they laughed and shouted over the music, got up in a group to dance and left me at the table alone. Hazel danced, too, but only a couple of songs and then "This is stupid," she said to me. She wasn't frowning, her face was blank, but I could tell she was mad, more than mad. "Let's just go."

Dia came back to the table as we were putting on our coats. "Aren't you having fun?" she said to Hazel. "Don't you know how to have fun anymore?"

"I've done this," Hazel said. Or did she say "I'm done with this"? Again, to me, "Let's go."

"Going home to open your Christmas presents?" Dia said. "Your new Burberry tote bag? Your butterfly charm?"

"Go to hell," Hazel said.

"Nice to meet you," Dia said to me; she was laughing.

Outside it had gotten colder; the cab was freezing and smelled bad. People were dashing around crazy everywhere, the stores were still open and frenzied for Christmas Eve. Hazel hunched against the window, staring out. I wondered if she was angry at me, or ashamed of me; I wanted to say something but I didn't know what. And I was angry, too, that those girls thought they knew what I was, who I was, just by looking, they hadn't even given me a chance. *BBG, so precious.* What did any of that have to do with me?

"Stop here," Hazel said to the driver, and we got out by the goat-cheese store, just a few blocks from home. She lit a cigarette and we walked, neither one of us saying anything. Finally "I'm sorry," she said.

"For what?"

"For the whole thing. It was a bad idea. I thought—"

"What?" but she wouldn't say what she thought, just walked and smoked and "Wait," I said, "my shoes," were killing me, too-high heels, it was too cold to wear shoes like that outside; I should have worn my Blondy boots, would they have made fun of those, too? but "Sorry," she said again, and slowed down. Our steps fell into a rhythm; a rhyme. We passed the sidewalk Christmas tree lot, LAST CHANCE!! scribbled on a piece of cardboard, a few skinny trees still left to buy. The pocket park was closed. One of the bodegas was blasting carols, "Silent Night," I started laughing and then Hazel started laughing, too. We laughed so hard we had to lean against the wall and "I'm deaf," Hazel moaned, mashing her hands against her ears. "Oh god I'm totally deaf, I'll never hear Santa come now."

"SI-lent night," I shouted. "HO-ly night."

A guy came out of the store to yell at us, an old guy in a blue sweater: "Go home. It's Christmas Eve, go home."

So we did, down the block, up the steps, I slipped on a slick patch and almost fell, but I caught Hazel's arm just as she caught me. Inside, Elbow pogoed up and down for joy. There were some people over, having drinks; the Christmas tree glittered, there were fresh white roses on the piano. Duncan wore all black, black sweater, black pants like Hazel's, a heavy new black watch; he looked gorgeous and kind of scary. Magnus wore a blue jacket and jeans. When he saw us, he said, "You two. Back already?"

"It was stupid," Hazel said.

"*Si*lent night," I said, and we started laughing again.

"I hate to leave you here," Magnus sighed, "in the gulag," the drop-off spot before airport security, everyone lining up with their phones and bags, rain running smeary down the foggy windows. I dragged my bag behind me like a refugee, it was so heavy, even though Magnus was shipping back tons of stuff for me, almost all of my presents; they had all given me presents, even Duncan: a picture of Elbow barking, in a tiny black frame.

"Call me," Hazel said. "As soon as you can, OK?"

"I will," I said, trying not to cry. I wanted to cry. I wanted to stay, to go back to the apartment with them, to spend New Year's Eve, to do anything but go to Sea Springs. Hazel hugged me. I hugged her, felt her infinity bracelet cool on my wrist, she'd fastened it on me in the cab: *I want you to wear it.* I hugged Magnus, who hugged me back, then slipped some Cherry Hot into my coat pocket: "For the plane," he said.

Duncan stood behind us, arms folded; he looked like security, like a bodyguard. At the last minute he'd come along to the airport. Now "Have a safe trip," he said to me, and nodded, a brisk brusque uncomfortable nod. I thought of what he'd said on Christmas Eve. I would have hugged him, too, but I knew he wouldn't like it, so I just nodded back, like *I will.*

"It was a joy having you visit," Magnus said.

"I'll see you in eight days," Hazel said. "Don't get a tan or I'll kill you."

"I won't," I said, "bye," I said, and finally turned away, trudging forward into the line, the crowds of strangers as "Come on, Bone," I heard Duncan say, and "OK, Dookie," Hazel said back—

—and then I did cry, I couldn't help it, hot tears rolling down my face, crying and trudging until "Bye, Calla Lily!" and I turned to see Magnus waving, all three of them standing there waving—

—and I waved back, a huge wave, like I was on a cruise ship, an iceberg, waved and waved with all my might, until the line took me away.

Philip and Helen Noble

Mrs. Noble: *I have such wonderful, wonderful memories of my own years at Vaughn, so naturally when it came time for my daughter to go to school, there was really only one choice.*

Mr. Noble: *Vaughn is an excellent school.*

Mrs. Noble: *And it's so much more than just the academics, although of course Vaughn is a wonderful school, the students go on to the best colleges. But what I really cherish from my time there is the friendships I made, friendships I still have, some of them, some of us have been friends for—well, I don't like to say how long, but believe me, we go way back! One friend of mine, Alison Bechmann, I met in the second grade—*

Mr. Noble: *Lily does very well there, she's an excellent student.*

Mrs. Noble: *And she's made many many lifelong friendships already, I'm happy to say. Because, you know, those teenage years, hormones, you can be swept up in the wrong direction, it's so easy for a girl to get confused. A good foundation is what you need, the safety of strong boundaries, and tradition. And being surrounded by people who care for you. Vaughn is like a family that way.*

Mr. Noble: *And Lily—*

Mrs. Noble: *Which is why we were so delighted when Lily wanted to try the boarding experience, which is something that I had never done—I was a day student, and so was Lily up until this last year. But when she wanted to stretch her wings a little, we were delighted, weren't we?*

Mr. Noble: *Yes.*

Mrs. Noble: *And the dorms are just lovely, the girls decorate them with posters, and flowers, and these adorable little lamps—*

though I can't speak for the boys' side, of course! Vaughn is coed, but not the dorms, naturally. The girls and boys don't even eat to-gether until junior year. Which is something else I appreciate, as a parent. That whole aspect of socializing, you know, girls and boys together—the longer a girl waits to become involved in all of that, the better it is for her grades, her academic life. . . . Not that Lily doesn't have boyfriends, she's dating a really lovely boy, James Keller. We like him a lot, don't we?

Mr. Noble: *Yes.*

Mrs. Noble: *But her main focus is on doing well at school, at succeeding, making as much of her opportunities as she can. Not everyone is able to go to a school like Vaughn, you know, unfortu-nately, so the girls who can, understand that this is really some-thing special, something to cherish. If you asked Lily herself, she'd tell you exactly the same thing.*

Mr. Noble: *Vaughn is an excellent school.*

7. June

The sun and shade made the lawns a giant patchwork, the library windows shone with glare. On the steps of the Admin building, a pack of lower-school girls waited to take a tour, clustered around two teachers; one of them I didn't know, and the other, Mrs. Roche, looked at me, looked at me again, and smiled. "Oh, it's Lily Noble," she said. "How are you, dear?"

"I'm fine." I'd had Mrs. Roche for seventh-grade math; she used to give us watermelon Jolly Ranchers when we solved equations. Now she seemed small to me somehow, with her little round tortoiseshell glasses and her poppy-patterned blouse. And the lower-school girls looked—not small, they weren't small, most of them were as tall as I was, and some of them had fairly huge chests already. But they looked really . . . young. Maybe because I was fifteen, thirteen was like another country. Another continent.

Mrs. Tai poked her head out of the building, squinting and smiling, nodding for the girls to come in. I remembered going on that tour, the freshman tour, even though I'd thought I already knew everything there was to know about Vaughn. I remembered whispering and joking with Julia, and Keisha, and Melissa Marquez, who was in our group but then moved back to California in the middle of the year; her dad took her out of Vaughn, and we all cried, and promised to keep in touch, but none of us ever did. Now all of those friendships seemed so—slight.

The night before I went to Sea Springs, Hazel and I stayed up talking about everything, life, and school, and the Bertram girls at the club: *Those sorry bitches,* Hazel said, *I can't believe I ever hung out with them. You think people are your friends. . . . They weren't my friends.*

I am, I said.

I could hear Elbow, breathing on the bed, a tiny high whistling sound. And she looked at me, and she smiled.

Now the lower-school girls clustered around the Admin lobby, murmuring, giggling. Disbursements was fortunately empty, just me and the lady who worked there; her name was Mrs. Finch. I said, "I want to close out my account, please."

She swiveled away from her computer. "For the summer, you mean? Well, we can put the full balance on your card now, and deactivate the account. But in the fall, your parents will need to reinstate—"

"No, I mean I want to close it out completely. Close it down."

"We don't close accounts for active students. Your

name is—?" She gave me a look through her blue-tinted glasses, then "Are you all right?" she asked in a different voice, like a mom, not an office person; she got up out of her chair. "Are you—"

"I'm fine." I could hardly see through the tears. "I just, I want to close out the account."

She didn't say anything, she handed me a tissue, fluffy pink. Then "You might change your mind," she said. "It's always better to wait."

"I won't," I said.

"Wait," she said.

Ms. Holzer's room was stifling, as hot as the dorms, even though she had all the blinds closed against the sunlight. That was the other medieval-ness of Vaughn, the inability to get the air-conditioning to work right. "It's awful in here," I said from the doorway.

"Just be glad you had my class first semester," Ms. Holzer said. Her hair was pulled back away from her face; she had a new bracelet, little golden links that looked like keys, or maybe they were keys; I didn't keep track, I didn't wear that style anymore. Just my infinity bracelet. "Can I help you with something, or—?"

"Hazel asked me to pick up her journal," I said. It wasn't entirely a lie, or it wasn't a lie to Hazel anyway. Ms. Holzer pointed to a file-folder box on the table past the horseshoe: there was a lot of stuff in there, forgotten papers, a couple of day planners; one was Constance Brill's. I flipped through it, the creased and dog-eared pages, a million sticky notes, her scribbly handwriting; it all went blank in mid-March. Hazel's notebook journal was close to the bottom, HJT scratched white across the Vaughn logo. She'd gotten a 92 overall. I think I got an 80. Keisha had gotten an 84 and filed a protest. "How is Hazel?" Ms. Holzer asked, but she wasn't looking at me, she was looking at her laptop, frowning at something on the screen.

"She's fine," I said. I took the journal and left, heading down the long path to the hockey rink, past the lacrosse field, past the theater; you could hear the orchestra inside, rehearsing for Convocation: "Hymn to Sweet Unfoldings," they played it every year. I wished I'd brought along some music, too.

If I had a Music to Your Ears soundtrack, these songs would have been on it:

Milagros—"Sweetness"
Tica Coover—"Everything You Think I Am"
R.E.M.—"Nightswimming"
Private Demons—"Let's Not Let Go"
Sexxton—"Give Me a Sign"
United States of Her—"Winter World"
The Sisters—"Get Away with Everything"

—because that was what I wanted, to get away from everything, to just *go*. Somewhere. Maybe not even school at all—maybe I could do work-study someplace, maybe with Magnus at Music to Your Ears, researching songs or something. Or as a dog walker. Or gluing symbols to model mannequins, like hieroglyphics, like a message in a bottle, "Please send help," how stupid was that? A lot of girls, most girls, would love to have my life. I used to love to have my life. Or at least I didn't think about it all the time.

At the Christmas Eve party, one of Duncan's artist friends—he looked like an artist anyway, red hair and red glasses, a silver circle pin on his jacket—started chatting with me: *You go to Hazel's school, right? The Vaughn School? A friend of mine used to teach history there, it's great, isn't it?*

It's OK, I'd said. *Academically and everything, it's excellent. Don't you like it?*

I'd shrugged, I didn't really know what to say. *No, it's just—I've gone there all my life, you know?*

And Duncan, by the piano, looked at me and said, *Maybe it's too small for you now.*

I sat down under the trees across from the hockey rink entrance, the grass pricked and tickled my legs. Hazel's *Franny and Zooey* journal started halfway down the page, her rushed and scrawly writing: *My name is Seymour, I'm the oldest brother in the Glass family. I have been dead for seven years. My little brother Zooey has an ulcer, and my little sister Franny prays all the time. This is one f-'d up family. Is it time for an intervention?* No matter what, Hazel could always make me laugh.

• • •

That night, I dreamed of flying, swimming through the deep blue air like it was water. When I woke up it was still dark, just about four a.m. I put on my swimsuit, took a bath towel, and headed down to the river. That little piece of bent plastic was a miracle: you'd never think it would work, but it did.

Swimming in the river was nothing like swimming in a pool, or even the ocean. Warmer than you'd expect, a current, not a tide, and every few strokes you'd brush up against things, or things would brush up against you. That's why it was better to do it in the dark. And that weedy, woody, growing smell, what was the word for that? Julia would know, actually, she had the largest vocabulary of anyone I knew, even though she hardly ever used it. A secret smell. . . . And when I swam this way, I was alone, completely alone on this campus of who knows how many people, kids, teachers, workers, Julia and Kells and Edward Flowers and Hazel, even Hazel wasn't part of it, this was only mine. Stroke by stroke, all the way to the bridge and back. Twigs in my hair, heat in my muscles, my shoulders, going against the current now, back to where my towel made a pale spot on the dark dewy grass. The sun wasn't up yet, just the blur of false dawn, but the birds were already starting to sing. When I climbed up the bank, toward the line of evergreens, I felt a peacefulness, as if the river had washed me empty, as if everything I didn't need had floated away in the dark.

8. February

"It gets worse every year," Mrs. Alwin said into the phone; she sounded phenomenally irritated. "And it's a major distraction, when what they should be concentrating on is exams, not— Yes, Lily, can I help you with something?" Mrs. Alwin had me on her Do Not Fly list for real now, she was always checking up on me, asking me what I was doing, if she could help me with things.

"Just getting my mail," I said. There were two letters in my box, one from my Nana—a Valentine's card, she sent me one every year—and a postcard reminder from the doctor, TIME FLIES! with a grinning bird on it, CALL FOR YOUR SPORTS PHYSICAL NOW! As I stepped out of her office, here came Julia, red binder jammed under her arm, giving me this brisk little nod like she was much too busy to stop and talk, too caught up in the drama of the hearts.

It was another one of those Vaughn customs, the Valentine hearts. There were two kinds: red cinnamon hearts in a heart-shaped box, for boyfriends or girlfriends, and the regular multicolored "conversation" hearts for everybody else, friends or teachers or coaches or whoever, to show your appreciation. On the surface it was for charity—that year it was a rain forest thing—so equally of course Julia was in charge of it, and "She'll get a ton," I said to Hazel in the hallway. "And she'll send even more. That's what a First Scholar does." But that didn't mean anything, except maybe to the people who were so far down the ladder that any kind of notice from Julia Baumgarten was a big deal. To me, there was no point in sending the things if they didn't signify at least *something*. Which was why I gave Hazel Cherry Hot instead of hearts, of course I would give her Cherry Hot; she gave me some, too. But I gave her hers first. . . . Why did I still think things like that, measure like that? Was it the memory of her yelling at Duncan: *I didn't even want to go there in the first place. You're the one*—who sent her here; kept her here? in the shadow of Lady Vaughn, *I said I would come for a year. One year. And I don't really care if I stay or not.* She cared now, though, didn't she? Cared about me? *You think people are your friends.* But what if she went into another "blue period"? What if—

"Hey," Hazel nudged me. "Look where you're going, woman, you're going to walk into the wall."

"I got dizzy," I said. "All the Valentine love in the air."

All day it was *the* discussion, in class, lunch, everywhere, who got what kind of hearts from who. Hazel gave a box of the regular hearts to Mr. Khalil, whose class she was loving (*Of course I love it,* she'd said, *Urban Patterns, come on, I could practically teach it!*). I gave a box to Ms.

Nell—she got a whole tower of them, more than any other teacher—and one to Mrs. Beebe in the dining hall, who acted like it was a bouquet of roses: "Well Lily, this is nice! What a nice girl you are." Alonzo was watching, and some of the other kitchen people, watching and smiling and "No," I said, "you, you do a lot here." I was embarrassed; it was just a dumb little box of candy. Maybe no one had ever given her one before.

Hazel did the best thing of all, deputized Magnus to go to the Sweetheart Shop, and send some dark chocolate hearts that were "Just rude," Edward Flowers told me, stopped sideways on the bike path; his eyes were shining. "They say stuff like 'This Sucks' and 'Why Me?' She's so insane. . . . She bungeed them to my bike seat. I'm surprised the raccoons didn't get them."

"What kind did you give her?" I asked, teasing. I'd already seen it was the red ones, wrapped up with red paper roses; Hazel had showed me.

In our class, Julia got the most red ones for a girl, of course, and Patton got even more, one box from a freshman boarding girl he didn't even know, but looked up—and hooked up with, people said—afterwards. Julia was furious: "She comes from *Kansas*, or someplace. She's a sad pushy little whore."

"Maybe she just wants to save the rain forest," Keisha said. Everyone snickered a little, even Audrey, who had sent red ones to Kells, I knew. He'd sent me red ones, the heart-shaped box left in my mailbox; had he tried to come see me? or timed it for when he knew I'd be gone? No, that was too subtle for him. And he probably didn't even know what my schedule was, we weren't in each other's orbit anymore. . . . I didn't give him anything, any kind of hearts. The red ones were a lie, and the other kind seemed mean, like throwing it in his face, *Let's be friends* when I knew perfectly well we wouldn't, we were never technically friends in the first place.

The only good thing about the stupid hearts was that it brought everything between us to the surface, which wasn't "good," but it was better than dragging on the way we had been, me making more and more excuses for why I couldn't see him, and him getting more and more frustrated, bouncing back and forth between sad and surly, sending me all these angry misspelled messages—*u think u 2 good r sumthin*—and then catching up to me on the paths, holding my hand, acting like nothing was wrong. When we hooked up it still felt all right—Kells was still a great kisser, he was the best kisser I had ever been with—but one of us always left immediately afterwards, and most of the time it was me. All of the time it was me.

And then that night, Valentine's night, the hockey game. . . . I had stopped going to watch him play a long time before, I just couldn't see the point. Crammed in at the rink, sweating and suffocating, then waiting forever in the cold for him to come out and walk back to Peacock with me, or me back to Crane with him, or stop off for some groping on the path—no. Besides, I didn't care about hockey, it just wasn't a sport I was into. Which wouldn't have mattered, if I was into Kells. But I wasn't anymore.

Which didn't seem to occur to Audrey and Greer and Abby Feldman, who came straight from the rink to my room, loud and excited, asking me why hadn't I been at the game—

"And Kells was so phenomenal, he forced the game into double OT—"

"And that one shot? Their goalie like never even touched it?"

"I know! Kells is like pro, Lily, you should have seen it!"

"Why weren't you there?" Audrey asked me, her head to one side, like she was concerned or something, like I would have to be dying in agony to miss out on a hockey game, especially one where Kells was the big hero but "I have a lot of homework," I said, and didn't say anything else, trying to make the point that I was busy; which was sort of true, I *was* trying to get work done, especially since Hazel was off with Edward Flowers at movie night (they were showing *Love Story*) and I had an eight-page paper due in History, "Women's Rights in the 20th Century," I was almost up to Gloria Steinem.

Finally they took the hint and left, or Abby and Greer did. But Audrey doubled back to stick her head past the door again and say, very pointedly, "You really should support Kells more, Lily, it's what a girlfriend does. Especially on a day like today."

"Why? Because he won the game?"

"Well, that too. But it's *Valentine's Day*, it's the day you're supposed to be with the person you care the most about—"

"You were there," I said, and looked at her, just looked at her, and after a minute she backed out and shut the door.

Actually I was relieved that Kells had had such a great game, it would keep him busy all night, and give him something else to think about besides the hearts. But it was only ten-thirty when my phone started up; even though I turned it off, I knew he wouldn't stop calling. So I took a breath, let it out slow, and called him back.

He picked up instantly, loud and slightly slurry, I could tell he'd been smoking but this time it hadn't made him silly, just stupid, so stupid that we started arguing immediately about something even stupider, my ring tone for him. But we both knew why he was really calling.

Finally he said it: "Where the hell were you tonight? Everybody was there, the whole school was there. Auds said— And *everybody* has fucking homework, so don't tell me you—"

"Well, I do." *Auds said,* she just couldn't wait, could she, to scamper over there, wherever he was: still at the rink? Or in his room? Or outside Peacock, staring up at my window? There was frost on the glass, in swirls and patterns. My fingertips were so cold I could barely feel them. "And anyway, I don't go to the games anymore, you know that."

" 'You know that,' " he mimicked. "Yeah, *I know that*. I know that you don't care about me anymore, is what I *know*. You don't go to my games, you don't come to my room, you don't send me any fucking hearts—"

I didn't say anything. I knew I was supposed to, I was supposed to jump in or deny or argue or something; but I didn't. Someone hurried down the hallway in backless slippers, *slap-slap-slap*. I stared at the frost on the glass.

"Why don't you just tell me the truth, Lils? Huh? Why don't you just, just break up with me, if you don't want to be with me anymore?"

"All right," I said.

Silence. For a long horrible second I was afraid that he hadn't heard me, that I was going to have to say it again. But then "Lils?" and his voice sounded so—young, like a little kid's, a shocked little boy and "Lils," he said again. "Are you— Do you mean it?"

"James," I said. I kept staring out the window; I could see the outline of my face in the glass, ghost face, ghost girl. The ghost of the girl I used to be, the girl he really wanted. "It's probably better for both of us, really, it's probably better that—"

"*Fuck* you!" and he was gone, hanging up as I sat staring at myself in the glass. Happy Valentine's Day, I thought. How many times has this happened, people breaking up on Valentine's Day? It seemed like I should be angry, or at least upset, or at least with someone, with Hazel, so I could turn to her and say *Well, that's it, we broke up*. And she would say *You knew it was going to happen sooner or later.* And we would talk about it, and she would tell me about awful breakups she'd had, and I would tell her how civilized it had been with Benjamin Partridge, how we just gradually stopped hanging out with each other, no fuss, no pain, just a kind of dwindling interest that died on its own. But she was at *Love Story* with Edward Flowers. And I was here on my bed by myself, looking at my face in the frost and the dark, wondering if I should cry or something, wondering why I didn't feel like crying, glad in a distant kind of way that at least it was over and done.

But it wasn't. The next day everyone seemed to know, though I hadn't told anyone, only Hazel, first thing in the morning, as soon as I stopped at her room and "You," she said, and hugged me, one long arm tight around my shoulder. "Why didn't you tell me? Why didn't you call me?"

"You were with— You were at the movie."

"Not all night. And I could have left. I would have, if I knew." She tilted my face up. I knew I looked awful, I hadn't really slept at all, just kept dozing off and waking, dozing and waking, until I gave up and turned on the light and finished my stupid paper. At least Constance Brill wasn't there to make it all worse; her allergies were so bad now that she spent most of her nights in the infirmary. Sometimes I forgot I even had a roommate, except for all her crap piled everywhere.

"Was it bad?" Hazel asked; I nodded. "Are you really sad?"

"I'm sad that I'm not."

"Then it was time," and she hugged me again, and we went to get breakfast. We carried our bagels and café crèmes outside, into the furious sunlight, the white dazzle of sun on snow, to perch on the steps of the Admin building, the steam from the cups floating sweet in our faces. And she didn't ask me about it anymore, or dissect it, or drown me in sympathy. Instead she told me all about Edward Flowers and *Love Story*, a stupid weepy chick flick, how she called him "Preppy" afterwards like the girl in the movie, and he called her "Jenny," but forgot halfway home and started calling her "Annie," so she called him "Sandy," like in *Little Orphan Annie*, that musical. And they stood by the doors of Peacock for half an hour, eating all the dark chocolate hearts, Edward Flowers entertaining her with *Love Story* trivia, like how every year the Cornell band played the movie theme song when its hockey team hosted Harvard, to mock it, because Cornell and Harvard played in the movie, or something—but "Oops," she said, and made a face. "Hockey. Sorry."

"I don't care," I said, and though it wasn't totally, entirely true—Kells had been my boyfriend for a long time—still it *was* true, I didn't care, not in the way that I was crushed or furious, not in the way that people expected. And people *did* expect, and speculate; I'd walk into a room and everyone would glance at me, it went on all day long. Even Constance Brill knew. Even the teachers: Mrs. Parais patted me on the shoulder, and Mr. Haywood gave me a chilly look in the dining hall. I didn't even have Mr. Haywood.

Finally Julia came up to me, as I was getting ready to go to the pool and swim laps, hoisting my bag on my shoulder and "Lils," she said. Audrey was behind her, and Greer behind Audrey. They all had the identical look on their faces, a kind of cosmetic concern. "We heard about you and Kells. What happened?"

I closed my locker door carefully. "If you already heard, you already know. We broke up."

"But what *happened?*" Julia pressed a palm to my locker, leaned in closer. "You two were so perfect together." Audrey's gaze flickered just a little when Julia said that, but her expression stayed the same. "And on Valentine's Day and everything. Why didn't you call me?"

Hazel had said the same thing, *Why didn't you call me?* But the difference was, she meant it: because she wanted to be with me, to help me; because she was my friend. Unlike Julia, who cared about Julia, period, who just wanted to know the gossip, to be able to tell everyone *I talked to her right afterwards, and she said* . . .

So "What were you going to do about it?" I said to Julia, my hand tight on the strap of my bag, thinking of all the years we'd hung around together, all the things we'd done, adding them all up to realize they didn't make much: I could have done those things alone, or plugged in Audrey for Julia, or even Greer or Abby Feldman, and it wouldn't have mattered, it wouldn't have *changed* anything. And that's what made me angry, not that she was pressuring me for details so she could run off and tell people, tell Kells probably first, Audrey would do it if she didn't, Audrey was just like her. Not me. Not ever, which meant I'd been wasting time, all that *time* so "What do you care, Julia, really?" I said, face-to-face with her, her eyes getting wider, then narrower as I talked. "It's between me and Kells, isn't it? And nobody else? And it's over. So why would you want to know anything at all?"

"I thought," pursing up her lips—in that second she looked exactly like her mother, *exactly*, you could even see where the lines would be—"that you might want to share it with me, like a friend."

"Are we friends?" I said, deliberately.

There was a long pause. Audrey's face was absolutely still. Greer's goldfish gaze went back and forth, back and forth until "Apparently not," Julia said. "Apparently you don't want anything to do with anyone anymore. Except your ghetto friend."

And I laughed. I didn't know I was going to, it surprised me, and it certainly surprised Julia. And once I laughed I was free, I wasn't mad anymore, I didn't care anymore so "That's right," I said. "You're right as usual, First Scholar. Just me and my ghetto friend, that's how it is."

Audrey leaned back and away, her arms folded; she

looked satisfied, as if this was what she'd hoped would happen. Greer just kept looking back and forth. "That's not going to help you," Julia said, cold.

It already has, I thought, but I didn't say it, I didn't have to say anything, all I had to do was wait for them to realize we were done, all done—and finally they did, Julia did, turning as Audrey and Greer turned with her, three of a kind walking off down the hall as I went the other way, outside into the afternoon chill, the bag's strap pleasantly heavy on my shoulder, breathing in the fresh cold air. The trees were dark like charcoal lines against the sky, the bushes were topped with snow. The shoveled brick of the paths was the color of a folded rose. For those minutes, as I walked, crunching snow, I was as happy as I had ever been at Vaughn. And I thought, It's over with, it's all over now.

But I was wrong. Stepping out of the girls' locker room in the natatorium, tired from all the laps—I'd swum longer than I should have, but it was a good kind of tired, where your body takes over from your brain—when "Lils," from around the corner, a guy's voice, for a second I thought it was Kells and my heart sank. But it was Patton.

He had his hockey jacket on; he had just come from outside, the cold was still on him. "I've been looking for you all day," he said. "My man Kells is in bad shape, Lils, he is fucked *up*. So what the hell happened with you two?"

I had to look up, he was so tall, tall like Hazel. The curving hallway was dim and bright, dim and bright, the shadows or the recessed spotlights. Past us, through the bluish glass, was the empty pool. No one else was around.

"Ask him," I said.

"I don't have to, it's all he can talk about. 'Lils left me.' What happened, girl?" in that Patton way, superior and intimate, like he knew all about you, like you were a room he could walk into anytime he wanted to, and touch anything he pleased.

"We broke up," I said. "There isn't anything to say."

"Lils, baby, it's OK." And he stroked my cheek, one long cold finger, soft and slow and lingering down the side of my face, tracing the damp curve of my jaw, ending at my lips and "Don't worry," he murmured. "I won't tell him." And we both knew exactly what that meant, it meant *I won't tell him because I want to hook up with you. Let's hook up.*

And I felt—it was kind of horrible, but I felt a little . . . tickle, an answer to his touch, his finger getting warmer on my mouth, and I—wondered. Just for a second I wondered, me and Patton, what would it be like—

—but in the very next second I was disgusted with myself, with him and "God," I said, stepping back, away. "You're supposed to be his best friend."

"I am." *He* wasn't disgusted, he would have hooked up with me right there and then, right in the hallway, and never felt bad about it for two seconds, because friendship was friendship and sex was sex and Kells and I were broken up anyway, right? He even said it: "You two are zero now, right? So—"

"I have to go," I said, and slipped past him, dim and bright and the door and gone; and he let me go, he hadn't been trying all that hard anyway. And if I said anything, if I told anyone, he wouldn't even have to deny it. There was nothing I could prove, it would look like wishful thinking on my part, or as if I had broken up with Kells to try with him. *Right there by the girls' locker room,* he would tell people, eyebrows up, like could he help it if girls threw themselves at him? And people would call *me* names.

The only ones I told were Hazel, and Edward Flowers, neither of whom was surprised, Hazel even laughed: "Man whore," she said. "It figures." And Edward Flowers patted me on the shoulder: "Congratulations, you're the only girl in the history of the Vaughn School to say no to Patton Ponder. *Any* Patton Ponder. There've been like seventeen of them, you know."

"And they were all freaks," I said. "Who wants to walk with me to Lady Vaughn? I think she needs a Valentine's heart, or a cigarette, or something."

"I think you need a bike ride," Edward Flowers said. "A midnight bike ride, come on."

That was the day we stole the bikes, not "stole" really, just popped the locks and rode them through the snow and the dark; I must have fallen over five times, I was laughing so hard. Hazel grabbed a bike that was way too small for her, but she kept on, her knees churning high, like a clown's. Edward Flowers offered me his bike to ride, his LeMond racing cycle, but I refused to even get on anything that complicated.

"That bike is smarter than I am," I told him.

"Not by that much," he said, and I rubbed a handful of snow in his hair.

That was the day I knew that Edward Flowers was my friend. He was in love with Hazel, utterly, but he was my friend; he liked me, we could talk to each other. I hadn't ever had a boy for a friend before, not since I was a little, little girl.

And he got to be friends with Alondra, too, and Devi, and Keisha, who already thought he was hot, but "Downtown's got him locked up," she said; that was her new name for Hazel, "Downtown." "But he's still the best dancer in this school. And everybody's fair game on the dance floor."

Oddly, after Julia and Audrey and all of them decided to cut me off, Keisha decided to come back; and she brought along Essi Lafamian, who none of us had really known before, one of those day students you see everywhere but never actually talk to. It turned out Essi was funny, in a very dry, Keisha-like way; and she could do a perfect impression of Mrs. Alwin, even better than mine. Hazel and Alondra ended up picking her for a partner in their Urban Patterns "My City" skit, to play the bewildered tourist. Alondra was the homegirl. Hazel was the narrator, and wrote the script. They got an A plus, and Mr. Khalil had them perform it again for the whole upper school, he said it was the best skit anyone had ever presented in his class. All the boys whistled when Alondra came strutting out in her miniskirt and sunglasses, and everybody laughed when Essi said, in this funny made-up accent, "Your customs are so *strange* to me"—everyone except the Julia crowd, who smiled, but only at each other: Julia sitting next to Patton, and Audrey sitting next to Kells.

Seeing him was—sad, I guess, because he refused to look my way, if his gaze ever touched mine by mistake he jerked his head around, like I was contagious, or contaminated. Of course he was already hooked up tight with Audrey, it had barely taken a week, which in a weird way made me really angry, the first time I was angry about any of it, but *"Que será,"* Hazel said.

"What does that mean?"

"It means 'whatever.' It means Audrey Zhang's been locked onto him like a heat-seeking bitch missile for months, and you don't want him anymore, so what difference does it make? Let her have him. It's not your problem anymore."

"I only wish he had better taste," I said, and just at that second, Audrey lifted her face for Kells to kiss, which he did. There was no way she could have heard anything, we were ten rows apart, but still. . . . They looked good together, I had to admit, like a matched set of something, something you run out to buy but never actually end up using. So I turned my head away, looked at the sun through the high square windows, looked at Mr. Khalil emoting onstage, looked at the butterfly on my charm bracelet, I'd have to take that off. Butterfly kisses. Whatever. *Que será*.

9. June

"Mrs. Parais?"

This art room was bigger than Mrs. Parais's room: more tables, more sinks, and more junk. And the whole front wall was a showcase, the door off to one side, ART ROOM/MORRISON in wavy burned-in script. I hardly ever came to this part of campus, the boys' upper school, equally blue-and-ivory but with a definite boy feel, that lawless-jungle-testosterone thing in the air. Their art was different, too: no papier-mâché vases or perspective drawings, and definitely no vestals: for their collage project they had posters, like old-style movie posters from the '70s or something, action heroes and cars and comic book explosions. One poster showed two guys skiing down a mountain of money with DOWNHILL SLIDE in jagged, cut-up letters across the bottom. At the very back of the room, a tall boy was doing something complicated with a big spindle of wire.

"Mrs. Parais?" I called again. "Is she here?"

Mr. Haywood had told me Mrs. Parais was in the art

room, but maybe there was another art room somewhere in this building? Or maybe Mr. Haywood told me the wrong thing deliberately? because he had been fairly cold to me ever since I broke up with Kells. As if it could ever be his business. Sometimes the teachers at Vaughn got a little too involved. . . . I'd seen Kells on the way over here, I waved, and he waved back. He didn't hate me anymore, he was happy with Audrey; like Hazel said, *Those Tropical Passion condoms really get the job done.* He and Audrey were in charge of leading our class into Convocation, and reading the Sophomore Farewell; every upper-school class had to give a Farewell. Keisha was writing ours. No one knew why Patton and Julia weren't giving it, or at least none of our friends knew. But it was obviously something they'd all decided together, those two and Kells and Audrey. And Mrs. Baumgarten, she was this year's parent liaison. . . . The whole thing was a little bit much, Convocation. Maybe next year they'd have everyone wearing costumes or something.

I called again—"Excuse me!"—and this time the boy looked up, looked back toward the door and "Oh," he said. "Sorry, didn't hear you." He had a little accent, or maybe it was just a way of talking, clipped and slurred. He was dark and tall and bony and dressed in dark blue, blue pants that looked like jeans but weren't, and a dark blue T-shirt. He reminded me of someone I knew but couldn't quite place. "Give a hand a minute?"

"What?"

"I mean, little help?" so I walked back to where he stood with the spindle, and I saw it was part of a guide-wire, looped around a robot-looking thing on the floor. He was trying to get it to stand upright but "Legs keep going," he said. "Just hold that a second—right, right—" transferring the spindle to my hands as he stood the robot straight; it was a lot heavier than it looked, I had to hang on hard while he struggled to lock the legs into place until *"There,"* as the weight left the wire, the spindle went light in my hands—and suddenly he smiled, a bright sweet smile that changed his face and "Sorry," he said. "I mean thanks. Thanks and sorry. Jermaine made the limbs, and Jermaine? *Not* mechanical."

"It's OK," I said, looking for something to wipe my hands with, the spindle and wire were oily. He gave me a wad of paper towels. "Mrs. Parais isn't here, is she?"

"You must be strong," he said, still looking at my hands. "What?"

"I'm trying to find Mrs. Parais," but by then I really wasn't, by the time I got back to our art room it would practically be dinner, I had to get my vestal done today no matter what so "Never mind," I said, and turned away, looking for someplace to toss the paper towels but "No no," he said, "no listen, who you looking for? If she's here, we'll find her. If she's not, we'll make her—"

"I don't really want to *make* her," I said. "I'm having enough trouble just making my vestal."

"Your what?" so I told him, our collage project, *create*

the mannequin in a way that is meaningful to you and "Those?"
he said. "Those're awesome, I saw some setting up, Morrison uses us as slave labor, right? The police car one, with
the head, wow. Phenomenal."

"I know, my friend did that one."

"Who's your friend?"

"Hazel Tobias."

"Oh man I know her. I mean I know Flowers, you
know Flowers? And Gunn, and Lafamian?" who was Essi
Lafamian's brother, apparently, but I didn't know him, or
Gunn, "Gabriel Gunn, track and field, and he paints. . . . A
freshman," he said, when I still didn't know who he meant.
"He's in my class."

"What's your name?"

"Hepburn. Chris. Chris Hepburn."

"I'm Lily Noble."

"Oh I know," he said. "Flowers says— Um . . . I'd like to
see your dummy, no I mean, what's the name for it? Mannequin, right?"

"We call them vestals. Or virginias," which was actually
Vaughn slang for vagina, and I was suddenly embarrassed,
and he made a weird face, saying, "Well I'll probably be
handling those—" and then we both went quiet until he
laughed, a laugh like a sneeze that he couldn't hold in, and
I laughed too, and he said, "I mean they want 'em all up
for Convocation, the art projects. For the parents, right?"

"Right," I said. We both stood there, looking at each
other, smiling. His eyes were so dark it was like looking

into dark water, like the river, nightswimming. "Maybe I'll see you in the art room, then."

"Yeah. Or someplace else, right, movie night or something, you ever go to movie night? This week's *Breathless*, it's from the '50s or '60s or something, supposed to be funny, or— Right, you have to go now. Sorry."

"Don't be sorry," I said, and turned to leave, past the tables, the showcase wall and "OK," he called, "I'm not sorry, Noble. Not sorry!" and I waved, and he waved, and I walked away thinking What else is there at Vaughn that I never saw before? This boy, the boys' art room, Essi Lafamian's brother. What else? Secret underground passageways? A different Lady Vaughn, one who puts down her bow and arrow and parties at night with the vestals?— which made me smile as I walked into our art room, Mrs. Parais was there after all, sorting papers, looking harassed and "Did you see the class portrait?" she asked me, the one Ms. Nell had supervised: Ms. Nell had decided against using the Vaughn shirts, and instead had us dress in our own Vaughn "uniform," whether that was a sports thing, like Devi in her basketball jersey, or something from your favorite club or class, like Abby Feldman in her French Club T-shirt, or Alondra in dramatic black for Thespians, to represent whatever you felt Vaughn meant to you. Hazel wrote "Urban Patterns" across an inside-out blouse, in wavy black letters; it looked very cool but unfortunately you couldn't really read it in the picture. I wore Hazel's Vaughn T-shirt, as a little private joke.

"I don't think this came out very well," Mrs. Parais said, squinting at the proofs. "Ms. Nell was trying to be creative, I know, but—"

It's fine, I could have said, or *Our parents will really like it,* because both those things were true. But what I said was, "Does it really matter? I mean, it's just a picture. How a person feels about Vaughn isn't something you can see anyway."

Mrs. Parais looked up at me, her eyebrows slanting the way they did when she was about to tell you your project was insufficiently creative. She dropped the proof back into the collage of her desktop, pencils, folders, twisted-up crepe paper, a carryout coffee cup. "You know, Lily, you're the only one who hasn't turned in her mannequin yet. It's a quarter of this semester's grade, and—"

"I know," I said. "I want—"

"I can't give any more extensions."

"I know. I came to finish it right now, to turn it in in the morning."

"You've cut it very close. This isn't like you." I had kind of stopped noticing when people said that, stopped being surprised, but I did think, What *is* "like me"? How could they tell if something was "like me" now? How could I? Nightswimming was like me, and the infinity bracelet, and eating Cherry Hot; pranking with Edward Flowers, like with the bikes, or when we ordered those pizzas for the *Victor* staff. Being Hazel's friend . . . was like me.

Even the mannequin was like me, the more I worked

on it: deciding where the symbols should go, the last ones I had room for, not from the symbol sheet but stuff I had found in a magazine. It was all in French, which I don't really speak, but you could tell it was about fashion, kind of imaginary-poor fashion, where the guys are deliberately ugly, and the girls wear couture blouses and plastic bags on their feet, that kind of thing. One of the articles was illustrated with little people like you see on signs—DON'T WALK, SCHOOL CROSSING—those little cartoon figures with round heads and no feet, forming letters with their bodies, spelling out the designer's name, I guess, DERNIER CRI. I threw out half the letters and rearranged the rest into I NEED, then glued them carefully, letter by letter, from the base of the vestal's bald skull to the top of her spine, like some people have tattoos; it would have made an excellent tattoo. I NEED, black letters on my white skin, like the vestal's. Porcelain blond.

"Maybe I should get a tattoo," I said to myself, out loud without thinking, and Mrs. Parais made a noise; I'd forgotten she was still there. She looked at me, I looked at her, I bent back to my vestal. After a few more minutes she gathered up her papers, pausing at the door to say, "Leave the door open when you go. Mr. Moore's coming," meaning Mr. Moore the custodian.

"All right," I said.

"He's bringing the Shop-Vac."

"All right."

The art room was a good place when it was empty like

this, the quiet, the faint old-paint aroma mixed with the smell of the glue, the way the sunlight filtered in through the side windows like stage lighting, setting a mood. . . . If I looked out those windows, would I see Hazel? riding Edward Flowers's bike, walking the paths, nesting in? Edward Flowers was going to Japan for the first part of the summer, for a language intensive, then home, which for him was someplace out west, Arizona, or New Mexico, someplace with desert and endless blue sky but *Won't you miss him?* I asked Hazel. *Three months is a long time.*

Well, there are planes, she said. *He could get on one.*

Or ride his bike, I said, and we both laughed. We hadn't discussed what I was doing for the summer. . . . Hazel and Lily. Bone and Calla. Which one of us was Lady Vaughn? Was it neither of us? Or both? I dabbed more glue over the letters, coating them, making them shine, clear like tears. I NEED. That was something else new, too, not just *want* but *need.*

"You look phenomenal," I said to my vestal. "Even better than Hazel's." The vestal looked back at me with her decoupage face, her lips the last blank spot, a sealed-tight white smile, mysterious, like she knew something that she wouldn't say. The sun shone through the side windows. The desk phone rang once, twice, quit. I thought about what I wanted her to say for me, and just like that, I knew.

10. April

Right before my birthday, Constance Brill finally crashed. We had pretty much stopped speaking after Christmas break: all I wanted to do was yell at her—for her clumped-up tissues everywhere, her piles of junk, her wheezing, sniffling, constantly sad face—so I mostly said nothing at all. And she'd stopped asking me for help, with her papers, her computer, anything. She shuffled in, did her homework (or attempted to), and shuffled out at night to the infirmary with her tissue box and comforter. It was like living with a stranger, someone you knew just well enough to dislike.

So when Mrs. Alwin called me into her office, to "discuss" my "roommate situation," I didn't know what to think, especially when she asked me to shut the door, but "Constance Brill is leaving us," Mrs. Alwin said, as soon as I sat down. "She's not able to continue at Vaughn."

I could have told you that six months ago, I thought, but I didn't say anything. Acting upset would have been a lie, a Julia thing to do, but I did ask if Constance was OK, like with her allergies, and "That's part of it," Mrs. Alwin said; she sighed. For a minute I wondered what it must be like to be Mrs. Alwin, stuck in this crowded little office jammed with mailboxes and Lost and Found and a hundred blue-and-ivory sticky notes, her phone constantly buzzing—parents, other teachers, coaches; it must have been like being an au pair for a gigantic family. Or a jailer in a very nice jail. She hunted around in the stacks on her desk, then tweezed out a folded paper. "She left this for you."

The back of a flyer for the Christmas canned food drive, taped shut: a note. Typical Constance. "She's gone already?"

"She left this morning, yes. Someone will be in today to collect her things. . . . It's really too late in the year for another roommate, I'm afraid, unless something comes up. Will that be a problem for you, Lily?"

I thought of Hazel. "No," I said. "It's OK, I don't mind being alone."

At lunch I discussed it with Hazel and Essi Lafamian, who had had Constance in one of her classes and "Worried girl," Essi said, without much sympathy. "Always talking about failing out. Guess she was right to be worried, huh?"

"She'll be happier somewhere else," I said. "Somewhere without me in it." They laughed, but I felt guilty for a second, I had sounded just like Julia. There was something about Constance that always brought out meanness in me; I wasn't sure what it was. "She left me a note," and I pulled it out, slit the cloudy tape with my thumbnail. " 'Dear Lily,' " I read aloud. " 'This is my last night in our room. I wish we could of been able to be friends, but—' "

"But what?" Essi sipped her water. Hazel didn't say anything, just watched me, my face and "Read it later," she said. "I have to go to the torture chamber, want to walk with me?"

"I need food," Essi said. "I can't live on licorice, the way you two do," so she stayed in the dining hall as we walked to the gym, where Hazel was supposed to be running makeup wind sprints for "Punishment," she said. "Mrs. Dixon feels I don't really apply myself to physical fitness. I told her I didn't really think I was going to make physical fitness my profession. So, wind sprints. . . . So what did whatsherface really write? Constance?"

I showed her the note.

Dear Lily,

This is my last night in our room. I wish we could of been able to be friends, but you ovviously think I'm a big loser. That's alright. But I would of liked to make one true friend here. This is a very lonely school.

Bye & good luck,
Connie
P.S. Happy birthday. ☺

" 'Connie'?" Hazel said. "Since when is she Connie?"

"I never said she was a loser. I never said that." Her stupid blue crewneck sweaters. Her constant snuffling. Her constant suffering. "I never said—"

"I believe you," Hazel said. We walked in silence, the fragile warmth of the day strongest now in the noon sunlight, on the brick paths that looked warm and rosy, though if you touched them, they would still be cold. Very cold. *This is a very lonely school.* I thought of all the birthday cards in my room, I'd strung them from wall to wall on bungee cords: cards from Hazel, and Edward Flowers, and Alondra and Devi and Essi and Keisha, Ms. Nell, my parents, Nana and Papa, even Mrs. Alwin. My favorite, after Hazel's, was from Magnus and Duncan, mostly Magnus, but Duncan had signed it, too, a sharp scratchy scrawl. The picture on the front was of a girl walking through the rain, umbrella closed, letting the rain soak her, and inside Magnus had written *Calla Lily—May you be drenched in life this year! Happy Fifteen!* I thought of what Magnus might think of Constance Brill's note; of Constance Brill. Of me, trying my best to ignore her, being impatient to her, kicking through her notes and books and papers on the floor—

"Welcome to the gulag," Hazel said. "I hope no one stole my sneakers, I think I left them in the— Lily? What's the matter?"

"Nothing." I shivered. "It's cold."

On my actual birthday I woke up to flowers at my door: my parents had sent them, a giant spring bouquet of purple-blue violets and ivory tulips, it took me a second to realize my mother had tried to match the Vaughn colors. Couldn't she ever, you know, give it a rest? On the card she'd written *We'll bring your "real" birthday gift along with us,* meaning to Visitors' Weekend, which came two weeks after my birthday. She'd asked me in e-mails what I wanted, and I'd given her a list, the longest e-mail I'd written to her lately; in months, really. She wrote almost every day, and I answered once a week, or I tried to. But it was like more homework, all those e-mails, all those questions: Was I thinking of trying out for the spring play? Was I doing well in swimming? How was James?—since I hadn't told her about Kells, I'd figured what was the point. I did tell her when Nana sent me and Hazel the hobo bags, she'd been in Costa Careyes with Papa and *They just looked like you and your friend,* she'd written in her funny rounded handwriting. A black one for Hazel and a blue one for me, with braided drawstrings and a little gold clasp shaped like a ram's horn, everyone asked where we'd gotten them, even Julia.

And I didn't tell about the birthday beers, of course. That was a close call, too close almost to be funny, though we laughed about it after. Hazel had smuggled in the six-pack, she wouldn't tell me how but I think it might have been through Alonzo; it was where we drank them, by the dining hall, popping one after another—shotgun, that's called—in the dark and the chill, unseasonably cold half rain and half snow and "Pretend it's champagne," Hazel stage-whispered, her breath all beery, "make a toast," and we clicked cans and drank another. I was feeling floaty and silly, like a balloon, and we kept drinking and giggling, giggling and shushing each other, the foamy chewy taste of the beer, our ice-cold hands on the ice-cold cans until Edward Flowers coughed twice and loudly—the signal, he was our lookout—and in ten seconds here came Mrs. Bryce, the director, bundled up in a quilted red parka, what was she doing down by the kitchens? which is what she asked us, "What are you girls doing down here?" but "They're helping me," Edward Flowers said, coming around the corner toting a black trash bag. "I'm collecting recyclables for an extra-credit project. On waste disbursement."

"Cans," Hazel said, tossing the cans in the bag. The full ones made a thunking noise, had Mrs. Bryce seen that they were beer cans? It was fairly dark back there, by the Dumpsters, the sloping delivery ramp. "Aluminum foil, too, right?" Hazel asked, turning to Edward Flowers, who nodded; he didn't look at all nervous, he was a truly phenomenal liar.

"Right," he said. "And HDPE plastic. I was going to ask—"

"Mrs. Beebe," I said.

"Right," he said. I knew he had no idea who Mrs. Beebe was, but Mrs. Bryce couldn't tell. "I was going to ask her for the plastic, whatever she can spare."

"Well, Vaughn recycles almost everything," Mrs. Bryce

said; you could tell she was somewhat suspicious. But the wet wind cut sharp around the corner, which is what really saved us: it blew away the beer smell, made it just too wet to stand there anymore so "You'd better finish up for tonight," Mrs. Bryce said to Edward Flowers, who nodded, shouldering his bag, and we nodded, too, Hazel and I turning toward Peacock, Edward Flowers heading off down the path into the dark; he kept going, too, even after Mrs. Bryce went inside, that's how good a liar he was. And Hazel muttered to me in a strangled voice, "I think I peed myself back there," and I burst out laughing, I couldn't stop myself anymore.

Next year was the big birthday, Sweet 16 and all of that, I already knew I was having it at Sea Springs. This year was just kind of low-key, but I liked that. Alondra and Devi and Essi gave me the deluxe gift basket from La Coeur, all kinds of body creams, Ambrosia Perfume Oil, a foaming oatmeal-honey facial, Tress Mud, all of it. Hazel and Edward Flowers gave me a set of Dirty Dolls, like on SlipTV: Devendra and Diva and Dirk and, whoever the other one is, I always forget—Diana, right. They were posed all around my room, my single room now, Constance Brill's old bed just a mattress and headboard, all her clutter swept away, everything start-of-the-year clean again. Hazel bounced up and down on the empty bed, next to the gift basket, smelling like beer: "Now you have a single, too."

"I know," I said. I hadn't asked Hazel to be my roommate, I knew she'd say no, and anyway there was something kind of cool about both of us having our own singles, like two apartments in the same building. At 10:55 she said "Happy birthday" again and went back to her own room, and I curled up on my slightly spinning bed, the beer taste gone a little sour, and thought *I'm fifteen now.* Then I thought, *I ought to at least brush my teeth,* and take off my jewelry, Hazel's other birthday present, the one just from her: a choker, a row of dark red beads strung on a spidery black chain. Someone had made it by hand, you could tell: the chain was a little uneven, one of the beads was warped because it was *One of a kind,* Hazel had said, as I lifted it from the little box. *Just like you.*

Two of a kind, I said, and hugged her. *I love it, it's beautiful.* And it looked phenomenal against my skin, the dark chain and red beads, like a string of rosebuds, dark red roses waiting to bloom.

"Oh dear," my mother said, "where did you get *that?*" It was almost the first thing she said to me, as soon as she got out of the car. She leaned close, not to hug me but to squint at the necklace. "That necklace. It looks like stitches on your neck."

"Hazel gave it to me," I said. "For my birthday. It's nice to see you, too."

And then my dad was hugging me, a one-armed kind of hug that went on for a long time, weirdly long for him.

"Lily," he said. He sounded out of breath. Maybe he'd started smoking, too. "How are you?"

"Fine," I said. All around us, people were doing the same things, climbing out of cars or cabs, hugging their kids, criticizing their looks; I heard Zac Sklar's father say "I pay them to let you walk around like that? Jesus." The weather had seesawed the last couple of weeks, from frozen to unusually warm, it was almost sixty degrees but my mother was wearing a big coat, white winter wool with huge fur cuffs and "Where'd you come from," I asked, "the North Pole?" But it didn't sound the way I wanted it to, quick and funny, like Magnus would have said it, just bitchy and unkind, like Julia would have said it. Which was not a good start for Visitors' Weekend.

Julia and I did have a moment of truce, standing in line for the cookies and tea—the idea was you were supposed to "host" your parents, bring them their refreshments, show them around campus even if they'd been there fifty thousand times—and "Hosting," I said to Julia, who was ahead of me, "is like having a sleepover with your mother."

Julia rolled her eyes. "At least yours goes home. *My* mother's here every fucking week, she's *always*— Oh hi, Mr. Haywood. My brother's been looking everywhere for you—" meaning her brother Josh, who was in eighth grade and exactly like her, or like her and Patton's child, if they ever had one: abusive and perfect-looking and good at all sports.

My parents sat waiting at one of the café tables set up

around the main entrance, doing what they always did in public: my mother chatting away with anyone sitting near her, my father looking at a spot six inches above everyone's head. It was the first time I'd seen them since Christmas, since the big reaction, overreaction, at Sea Springs.

Not only was the holiday part a total disaster—they'd saved opening the gifts until I got there, which hacked off my greedy little cousins—afterwards all we did was fight, my mother and I, because *The only thing you can talk about is what a good time you had at Hazel's,* my mother had said. *As if there's nowhere else on earth to enjoy.*

For me there isn't, I'd thought, turning the infinity bracelet around and around my wrist, thinking of Elbow and the piano and the bodega and the park, of Hazel and Magnus and Duncan waving goodbye but *She's growing up,* my Nana had said, raising her comma-shaped eyebrows. *She'd rather be with her friends, what's wrong with that?* Then she'd asked me a bunch of questions about Hazel and Duncan and Magnus, all the things we did, the places they'd showed me and *"Calla,"* she'd said, *oh that's so clever and lovely. And you do look like a calla lily, don't you, darling.*

Maybe I should change my name, I'd said back, joking, and then my mother just completely lost it: *First you talk like her, then you dress like her, now you want to change your name? That is ridiculous, Lily, that is ridiculous,* getting louder and louder until I shouted back, and my Nana cried, and my father came in from the balcony to say *That's enough now.*

And then my mother had stormed off somewhere, probably to smoke, and I went down to the beach where my stupid cousins were throwing sand dollars at each other. Then Papa made us all go to some Cuban restaurant for a pointless five-hour lunch, where I called Hazel a hundred times but she never answered. And that was the way it went for six days. I was so happy to get back to Vaughn, I could have kissed the ground.

Since then my mother had sent me her every-single-day e-mails, and I'd answered back occasionally, but we'd never talked about Hazel. Knowing that they were coming here didn't make me happy, or make me miss them; I hadn't really missed my parents at all. No matter what else happened next year, at least I knew I wanted to get away from them. From her. . . . But first I had to live through this year; this weekend.

They used to call it "Parents' Weekend," but since it wasn't always the parents who came anymore—like the corporate kids sometimes had a rep instead; or Devi's mom and dad were still in Mumbai, so they sent her Uncle Vik from Boston; or Duncan and Magnus, who weren't coming till Saturday—Vaughn changed the name to "Visitors' Weekend." Which also meant they could piggyback in a day for "inquiring" students and their families, to meet Vaughn families, tour the campus, be shown around by student ambassadors that they handpicked.

This year, Hazel was actually one of them, she got an e-mail invitation from Mrs. Tai (*You've been chosen to share*

your enriching Vaughn experience with other young people) and
Why'd she ask you? I asked her. *It's mostly just seniors, isn't it?*
My stellarstudent record, probably.
No, seriously.
I don't know. She made air quotes. *"Diversity." I'm not
blond, I don't have a break tan from Boca. . . . It'll peel that red
dot off my file anyway.*
Do you really care about that?
She gave me a very Duncan-like look then, all stillness
and narrowed eyes: *Wouldn't you?* Only if I wanted to stay, I
thought, but I didn't say it.

So as I waited in the endless refreshments line, I
watched her, looking un-Hazel-like in a blouse and skirt—
all black, but still—and a pair of my flats, her feet were
slightly bigger than mine but she didn't have any shoes
that would work with that skirt—shaking hands with a
dad in a royal blue sport coat and a mom who was totally
overdressed, pink pantsuit, pouffy red blouse and pearls,
and their daughter, who was very tiny but otherwise
looked a lot like Hazel did when she first came, surly and
punk-rocky, the girl was even wearing tire-rubber sandals
with no socks. Hazel raised her eyebrows at me very
slightly as she led the family away, as I finally got the stupid tea and cookies, as Edward Flowers came up beside
me in khakis and a Vaughn tie, hands in his pockets and
"She won't stay," he said, and I looked at him hard but he
was looking at the girl, the family and "She won't," he said
again. "You can always tell."

"What do you mean?" I'd thought he was talking about Hazel.

"You know. The ones who won't ever fit in. Like the mothers wear 'nice' kinds of dresses, or weird pantsuits like that lady, and the fathers went to some hick college— Overdressed, you know? Over-everything. Like just getting here is a huge struggle. And then they do get here and find out, Hey, good luck, the struggle's just starting."

I thought for one second of Constance Brill. "So you're like a philosopher now?"

"Just a humble tour guide," he said. He'd asked to be an ambassador because Hazel was doing it, and his parents weren't coming until Saturday either. He was so excited about them meeting Hazel, it was really sweet. I couldn't imagine Kells wanting me to formally "meet" his parents, although I sort of knew his mother, and I'd met a zillion mothers exactly like her, the typical Vaughn-type mother. Like my mom.

Who took the tea and cookies as if she'd never had anything so delicious before, and thanked me like I was Mother Teresa—"This is really lovely"—so I wanted to smack her, or at least make her act normal, so "You've been to these things every year for the last eleven years," I said. "They always have the exact same butter cookies and tea."

And my dad just sat there, staring at his nonexistent point, hands clasped between his knees, until "Lily," he said, "we'd like to take you to dinner tonight. And your friend, tomorrow. With her parents."

"You mean Hazel?"

"That's right," he said. "We'll have lunch together."

"Brunch," my mother said. They weren't looking at each other. Obviously this was something they had argued over, but who had won? "Magnolia's does a lovely Sunday brunch, we can go right after the presentation."

"All right," I said, and then, because they seemed to be expecting more reaction—what was I supposed to say?— "That'll be good."

Then it was time for The Tour. But how can you show someone around when they've already seen everything there is to see, multiple times? So I decided to shadow Hazel and her newbies, which turned out to be kind of fun. The science wing, the art room, the upper-school library, the dining hall, she was doing a phenomenal job, pointing out everything they might need to know about, making them laugh, making Vaughn sound like Harvard and heaven rolled into one. And the little punk-rocky tire-tread girl had obviously fallen in love, she was just worshipping Hazel, asking a million questions: "Where's your dorm room? What classes do you take? Have you always gone here?" and Hazel smiled at her, at the parents, and said, "I've been very fortunate to be able to continue my education at Vaughn." And she let her smile stray over their heads, to me. I smiled back as "I'd like to see your room now," my mother said; was she trying to get us away from Hazel? or did she have some other motive, like getting the dirt from Mrs. Alwin in her office, a cozy little chat—"I'll just be a second"—but of course she wasn't, of course my dad and I had to sit around waiting, as other parents tramped up and down the hallway, trailing their daughters, sat there in my room where my dad looked around at the half-full half-emptiness and said, "You don't have a roommate?"

"She left."

"Why?"

"She was failing. And sick."

"Sick?"

"She had a lot of allergies."

"Oh."

He looked around some more: the piles of books and makeup, the birthday cards still hanging from the walls, the Dirty Dolls—Hazel had positioned two of them together on the dresser top, Diva humping Diana, we had laughed about it but all of a sudden I wondered if my dad was looking at that, so I stepped casually in front of the dresser, pointed at the window and "I've got a nice view," I said, which was a dumb thing to say even though it was true, but it made him look out the window, so I could tip the dolls facedown.

Then he looked back, at my nightstand and "What's that?" he said, pointing at the little black frame, Duncan's picture of Elbow barking and "That's Elbow," I said. "Hazel's dog." And then without knowing I was going to say it, I asked, "Why didn't we ever have a dog?"

He looked at me then, really looked, surprised. "Why? Did you want one?"

"I just— I always wondered. Don't you like dogs?"

"I like dogs," he said. "Weimaraners. They're so elegant, such an elegant animal. But you have to give time to a dog, attention, exercise. They get lonely just like people do. And bored. It isn't fair to keep them cooped up in a kennel."

Now I was the surprised one, that he would have thought that much about a dog, a dog's feelings, anybody's feelings. And that he liked Weimaraners, that he even knew what they were.

"Elbow is a mutt," I said, passing him the picture. "But he's really smart. When we took him to the dog park, he knew exactly how to press the drinking fountain lever to get water. And he knows someone is at the door before they even buzz."

He looked at the picture of Elbow. Then he looked at me, his lawyer-look, like he could see what you were thinking, even the thoughts you didn't know you had. So I turned away, toward the door as we heard my mother coming, her half-public, half-normal voice: "—the same page, absolutely. I know she's going to blossom junior year—" my dad setting down the picture as she stepped into the room, Mrs. Alwin pausing in the doorway and "Mrs. Alwin's invited us to dinner," my mother said, as if this was the treat to end all treats.

Actually it was even worse than I thought it would be. Pork medallions and lukewarm carrots, in the faculty dining hall that was actually just a smaller and less-nice version of our dining hall, and Mrs. Alwin in this awful tailored blouse-and-slacks outfit, *overdressed, over-everything*. Watching her, I wondered for a second if there were scholarship teachers, too, teachers who came to Vaughn to, like, better themselves? Was Mrs. Alwin one of them? and maybe Mr. Brown, too, *all downtown and hard-core?*

The whole dinner was my mother talking about how much I loved Vaughn, how it was my second home, and Mrs. Alwin nodding and agreeing; it was like being stuck in an infomercial. I sat there rubbing one foot against the other, my new chunky heels had given me giant blisters. And then, at dessert, Mrs. Bryce "dropped in," as Mrs. Alwin smiled all over the place, as I thought about the birthday beers and "The tours went very well today, I thought," Mrs. Bryce said. "And your friend did a lovely job."

For a second I didn't realize she was talking to me, talking about Hazel, until I saw my mother's mouth tighten, you could see the smoker's wrinkles, little lines drawn all around her lips but "The Lewandoskis made a point of telling me how impressed they were," Mrs. Bryce said. "Mrs. Lewandoski said that if her daughter turned out like Hazel Tobias, she would be very proud."

"Vaughn's a wonderful opportunity," my mother said, "for all kinds of girls. Like Lily."

Mrs. Bryce turned to me again. "I want you to know that we all appreciate the way you've taken Hazel Tobias under your wing. You're a real asset to Vaughn."

I didn't do it for Vaughn, I thought, but "Thank you," I said, because I knew that was what I was supposed to say. What would Hazel have said? The tire-tread Hazel would have made a joke about "ass" and "asset." The Hazel that led tours . . . ? What would Magnus have said? Magnus would have found a way to be nice, and mean it. I didn't mean it. What I meant was "Hazel's taught me a lot," so I said that next. My mother's mouth tightened up again. "*She's* a real asset to Vaughn, I think."

"Oh, we think so, too," Mrs. Bryce said.

Eventually it was over: the coffee, the date tartlets, my parents walking me back to my room, I thought I was finally free but "Time for your present," my mother said, perching on Constance Brill's old bed, reaching into her bag for a Tiffany box because they, she, had gotten me a new charm, a chunky gold heart, *Finally 15*, with a tiny twinkling diamond dotting the i, my name and birth date engraved on the back. "It's a keepsake," my mother said. "For your charm bracelet. . . . Don't you like it?"

"It's pretty," I said, because it was, in a Julia Baumgarten kind of way. "But—"

"But what?"

"Well, I don't really wear that bracelet anymore."

"Why not?"

"I just don't."

She looked at the infinity bracelet, at Hazel's birthday necklace; she looked me in the eyes. "I don't know who you're trying to be, Lily," she said, "but you are who you are. Don't forget that. You are who you are."

I set the box down. It was almost a relief, to get into it finally. "Why do you hate Hazel so much?"

"I don't hate anyone." Her voice got sharper. "But what you refuse to see is that Hazel Tobias comes from a completely different background than you do, she's a completely different kind of person. She's been raised without parents, bounced from school to school—"

"She has parents! She has Duncan and Magnus!"

"—in a totally unstructured atmosphere. Her life is nothing like yours. Nothing."

"We go to the same school, don't we? And anyway I don't care about any of that, her parents, whatever. She's my friend. She's my best—"

"I only want the best things for you. But you're trying to reject everything you come from, Vaughn, me, everything—"

"You can't make me be like you! You can't make me want what you want!"

My dad stood up. "That's enough now. Helen, come on. Lily, we'll see you in the morning." Right then my phone buzzed, I'd had it on vibrate all through dinner, Hazel hadn't called. Now it was Edward Flowers.

RIVR? he wrote.

They stepped into the hallway, my father said something to my mother that I couldn't hear. I stuck the Tiffany box in the drawer, and yanked off my chunky heels.

"Wow," Magnus said. His voice was cheerful, but a little hoarse in the chatter and noise, all the families crowding down the auditorium aisles. "You guys have a real Jackie O thing going here, huh? Charm bracelets over sweater sleeves, belted trenches, wow." He was smiling, teasing me, teasing Hazel who was in an unnatural mood, not acting out but not talking, either; like Duncan, actually, though I didn't point that out.

Duncan hadn't said two words to anyone, just sat there looking amazingly Heathcliffy and handsome in a black sweater and gray wool jeans; people—girls—kept turning to look at him, check him out, even Mrs. Flowers checked him out, Mrs. Flowers in her tasteful Chanel jacket and little white skirt, Mr. Flowers leaning over the seats, shaking hands with everyone until "Let's begin," said Mrs. Tai from the podium, the official welcome-to-Vaughn speech, everyone was there.

It was odd to see people matched up with their parents, especially if they were parents you didn't know. Like Greer Reinhardt's father, who looked nothing like her, he looked like Santa Claus, only blond. Audrey's style-section parents (who actually did look like her) sat next to Essi Lafamian's weird mother—not to be mean, but she really was kind of weird-looking, like from the 1960s or a villager or something, with peasant boots and peasant blouse and a peasant purse with yarn for a handle. Up on stage, between Mrs. Tai and Mrs. Bryce, Julia stood in her little black suit, nodding and smiling through their speeches, then working that First Scholar thing with her mother, saying this dialogue that was supposed to sound spontaneous but that, I knew, Julia had written out herself, about how Vaughn was a community of learners and leaders, of people who cared passionately about tomorrow and tomorrow's world—

"After all, it's going to be our world," Julia said to her mother, smiling.

"We're looking forward to watching you conquer it!" Her mother smiled back.

I glanced at Hazel, to get her to react, to whisper something to me, how could she not be laughing at this?—but she was staring at her nails, rubbing her nails back and forth across her knee. Duncan stared at the ceiling. Only Magnus was actually listening.

"Vaughn's our world, too," Julia said. "A world we're proud to represent," a world that crushed into the lobby as soon as her speech was over, everybody talking at once—

"—got Daddy wrapped so tight he's strangling, that's for sure."

"Oh he went to some state school, you know, where car mechanics go—"

"—sued them twice—"

"Last summer, you mean? When she was thin?"

My mother made a beeline for Mrs. Baumgarten, and gave Julia a little hug. Duncan and Magnus stood off to one side, talking, Magnus said something in Duncan's ear that made him smile, but when I said "What's so funny?" Magnus just winked, a friendly wink but he wouldn't tell me, as if I was a stranger or something, which made me feel awful; the whole morning was awful. They'd gotten in late—I guess Duncan had been on a photo shoot—and came straight from the airport, straight to the stupid assembly, without a minute to be with Hazel alone.

And then we all had to rush out to the overcrowded brunch at Magnolia's, where half the school had apparently wound up: Patton Ponder was by the windows with his parents; Audrey and Julia's families shared a table. At our table, I sat next to Hazel, with Magnus across from me, between Duncan and my mother, who almost as soon as we sat down asked Hazel how she "came to" Vaughn, like Hazel was Hansel and Gretel lost in the forest, following a bread crumb trail.

So Hazel started telling about her intake interview, all the questions they'd asked, about Bertram High School and her erratic test scores and "Then," Hazel said, "they asked me, Why do *you* want to go here? Not your family, you. And before I could even open my mouth, he pinched me," elbowing Duncan, who glared at her.

"No I didn't."

"Yes you did, you fucking pinched me."

My dad frowned—swearing! at the table!—my mother made a fake little laugh and "Well," Magnus said mildly, "it must have worked, because here you are," and everyone relaxed a little; he was so soothing, like aloe on a burn, maybe that was why he and Duncan got along so well. Although I noticed that they weren't holding hands like normal, or even really touching, another weird thing on a weird day where only Edward Flowers, last night, had made any kind of sense: meeting me at the river, walking back and forth behind the trees and *Hazel's all jangly,* he'd said, when I'd asked where she was, why she hadn't come with him. *I think it's because her brother's coming in, or something.*

We're all having brunch tomorrow, I'd said, *the happy families,* and he laughed, a musical sound in the dark. *My mother only ever wants to go to La Mer,* he'd said. *Thank God.* Then he'd looked back at Peacock, the lights on, Hazel's light and *She shouldn't take it all so seriously,* he'd said, serious himself.

But everybody seemed to be taking everything too seriously, my mother and the stupid charm bracelet, my father and the swearing, so Hazel swore a lot, so what? but for some reason it seemed to be bothering Duncan today, too. In fact for one odd second—looking at him, looking at my dad—they seemed exactly the same, drinking their coffee, picking at their duck scramble and wild berry waffles, so obviously wishing to be somewhere other than where they were; and Hazel, too, next to me but a million miles away. Not joking, not talking, we hadn't really talked at all since Thursday, since before my parents came and *What's your mom like?* she'd asked me then, lying on my bed, tugging a rope of Cherry Hot. *You look a little like her, in that yearbook picture thing. The mother-and-daughter party.*

That was such a fiasco. Everyone hated it.

So what's she like?

Nothing like me, I'd said.

Now my mother finished up her endless "funny" story about getting stuck on a lift at Vail or something, why would she even bother telling it? She can barely even ski, she only goes to Vail to see her friends. Then she excused herself to the ladies' room, and Hazel left a minute later, leaving me completely stranded. Magnus was trying to get some kind of pleasant conversation going, but between my dad and Duncan it was like reinventing the wheel—

"Do you ski, too, Mr. Noble?"

"I don't have time for sports."

"Oh, well, I'm not a big sports person myself. . . . Although Duncan used to speed-skate in college."

"Really?" I said. "Wow, what was that like?"

"Cold."

—so eventually I gave up too and went off to the ladies' room, fake cabbage roses and cotton-candy air freshener, but no one was there, just some old lady washing her hands for five minutes. So where was Hazel? Hiding in the men's room? Calling Edward Flowers? I stepped back into the hallway, heading slowly back toward the dining room, when I saw a little side exit I'd missed before: frosted glass doors leading to a tiny boxed-in courtyard, wrought iron benches, potted trees with no leaves—

—and there was Hazel, *and* my mother, smoking, both of them sitting there smoking.

For a second, a very long second they didn't see me, they were too busy talking, my mother talking and Hazel smiling, a funny kind of embarrassed smile, bouncing one foot up and down. My mother scooted next to her on the bench like they were best friends or something. And then my mother leaned forward and patted Hazel's knee, all Mrs. Hypocrite Nice Lady, what a total fucking *liar*—

—so I pushed at the doors, hard, and they saw me, my mother jumped up and threw down her cigarette as "What are you doing?" I said. My voice was loud in the little space. "What do you think you're doing?"

"Lily, listen to me. I haven't actually started again, I—"

"I don't care if you're smoking," I said. "That's your problem. And *Dad's* problem."

Hazel crushed out her own cigarette. "Calm down," she said, "who're you, Mrs. Alwin? Who cares if your mom smokes?"

"I don't. She can smoke all she wants to. What I care about is that she's a total liar."

"Hey, that's, that's fucking rude. You shouldn't talk to your mom that way."

"Don't stick up for her." I wasn't looking at Hazel, just my mother. "You don't know what she really thinks about you. What she says."

"*Lily.* Lily, stop it right—"

"She says—don't lie, Mom—she says we shouldn't even be friends. Isn't that what you said last night, *Mom?* You don't want me to be friends with Hazel because Hazel's too weird for me, Hazel doesn't have a family—"

—and Hazel's face changed, slammed shut as she jumped up, rushed out, past the glass doors and "Why did you do that?" I said to my mother, shouted at my mother. "Why did you have to do that?"

"Lily," my mother said. She looked shocked. "That was so unkind."

I had never been so angry with her in my life, never. I felt like throwing up, I was so angry. "Don't talk to me. Don't say one more word."

Back at the table, Hazel sat staring straight ahead, ignoring everything, Magnus's worried smile, Duncan's frown and "We should be getting back," my dad said, folding his napkin. He insisted on paying for brunch even though "You don't have to do that," Duncan said, unsmiling and "It's my pleasure," my dad said, not smiling either.

"Hazel?" I said, as we got up from the table, trailing behind her to the door. "Hazel?" She didn't answer.

In the parking lot, she climbed instantly into the rental

car without inviting me, without even looking my way and "Go home," I said to my parents. "Just drop me off, and go home," my mother at the passenger-side window, my dad giving me that extended one-armed hug again and "Call us if you need anything," he said, which if I didn't feel so extremely awful would have made me laugh, like, haven't you done enough? I couldn't see the rental car anywhere. And I was starting to feel a horrible sick hollowness, a fear that Hazel had misunderstood completely, that she didn't see it was my mother who was trying to ruin our friendship, that somehow she thought— But how could she not know what I meant? not know *me*? She knows me, I thought.

"Call us," my dad said again. I nodded, to make them leave, then trudged past the main lawn—the families gathering for the afternoon activity, some soccer game between the Vaughn varsity and the teachers—and headed down to the river, where I thought Hazel might have gone; but she wasn't there. No one was there, just the calm brown chill of the water, the clog and drift of last year's twigs and leaves pushed free by the end of winter. I sat there, watching the drift, listening to the shrieking and clapping from the soccer game, feeling more and more and more alone.

My parents are dead, I live with my brother, is that enough family for you? And I don't really care if I stay or not.
    I care.

• • •

Magnus sighed. "Come on, Calla." He handed me another tissue. "You've got to stop."

I turned my head to blow my nose; I sucked in the damp chlorine air. "I'm trying," I said. There were only a few families still touring the natatorium, almost everyone else had either gone, or gone to the dinner. "But she was so . . . awful."

She had been more than awful, she'd been nuclear, white-faced and fierce like at Christmas screaming at Duncan, only now she was screaming at me but *My mother doesn't know you,* I'd said, my back against the door, *she doesn't know anything about you. I know you! You're my best friend for life. I'm Calla and you're Bone—*

Don't call me that, don't ever fucking call me that! Miss BBG, Miss Burberry fucking Bitch Girl, what do you know about anything? All you know is this bullshit school! You and your bullshit mother!

"She was like a stranger," I said. "Or like I was."

Magnus sighed again. "She can get very gloves-off. Especially when she's hurt."

"But how could she think that *I* would think— I mean who *cares* who your parents are? What difference could it possibly make?"

"You can say that," Magnus said.

Someone let a door slam; the blowers cycled on. I wanted to dive into the pool, the turquoise water, the sea inside. "I don't know what to do," I said. I wiped my eyes with the disintegrating tissue. "What should I do?"

Magnus put his arm around my shoulders. He didn't say anything. I didn't say anything. We watched the empty pool, the ripples, the gleam of the overheads. Finally "Duncan told me," he said, still looking at the pool, "that Hazel was happy here."

"I know. I heard," after the assembly, waiting in the lobby for my dad to get the car, Duncan saying to Magnus that *It's worth the tuition, the—being away, all of it. She's nested in, did you see that? her room, and everything? Finally she's nested in.* "But she's changed since she came here. I mean, she led a *tour.* She never would have done that before."

"I know."

"Do you think she's—do you think she wants to stay here?"

"Do you?" he said.

"It was so nice to meet you," Mrs. Flowers said to Hazel and "You too," Hazel said back, holding her empty juice cup. Bagel wrappers floated by across the lawn, the dregs of the Sunday goodbye breakfast. The Flowerses were just about the last parents to leave, everyone else had gone already except the Baumgartens. Duncan and Magnus had left very early that morning, before I'd even come down. The weather was phenomenally nice, blue skies and puffy clouds, and warm, almost like summer. Edward Flowers was wearing brown-and-white beach shorts. Hazel was wearing pink aviator sunglasses. I hadn't slept all night.

Mrs. Flowers reached up—she was about two feet shorter than Hazel—and hugged her. Then she hugged Edward Flowers one more time.

"It was a lovely visit," she said to him. "We loved seeing all your friends."

"Have a good flight," Edward Flowers said, closing the cab door. "See you at Convocation," as they pulled away, sun flashing off the side-view mirror and "What a weekend," he said to us. "All those soccer games and singalongs in the chapel, god. It's like being in a movie or something. 'Your customs are so *strange* to me.' "

"No they're not." Hazel said, to him. But she was looking at me. Did she mean—what did she mean? I didn't know. I didn't ask.

Shelley Dixon

As a member of our transitions team, I see a lot of things, a lot of differing personal situations. Vaughn can be an amazing opportunity for a student, it can open so many doors in life, but what you have to keep in mind is that a kid is more than just her GPA. And even if she is a very bright kid, depending on the situation she comes out of, that may not be enough to succeed here.

I'm part of the Wilmington Scholarships team, too, and in that program we see a lot of kids who are just at the top of the heap academically at their old schools. But when they come to Vaughn, sometimes they struggle. Because it's not enough to be very bright, you know, that's just the starting point. Being bright only gets you in the door. And once you're inside, well. There are adjustments to make, delicate adjustments. And I don't mean only financially, although the Wilmingtons are offered only to students with financial concerns. I mean, these are kids for whom it's a struggle, sometimes, for Mom and Dad to pay the bills. It's a struggle for Mom and Dad to afford the lacrosse equipment, or the costs of winter break transportation, or whatever. So financial issues are definitely part of it, but they're not the whole story.

I lost one of my advisees this year—not to get too detailed, but she had a very difficult time keeping her head above water here. Money had nothing to do with her case. It was a combination of things, health issues, getting on top of her studies, getting out from under her loneliness—being a boarder in particular can be a lonely thing. And her roommate was not especially welcoming. . . . See, what a lot of these girls don't understand—and don't get me wrong, these are very nice girls, most of them, smart, friendly, kindly girls—but what the ones on the inside don't see is that there are very definite lines here, there are boundaries of who gets in and who doesn't, who's in and who's out. Sometimes it's as simple, in the lower grades, as what do you have? Do you have the latest device, you know, the newest phone or computer or whatever? Where do you go on break, do you go to Boca or Vail, or do you just stay home, or go to your grandmother's house or something like that?

The older ones, it's more about their own culture, you know, their own sense of belonging to something like Vaughn, to the culture that Vaughn represents. I don't want to get too anthropological here, but social class is an issue. Social class is definitely an issue, whether the girls put that name to it or not. And they don't. I don't see mockery or deliberate exclusion here, there's not a lot of "Oh, you're poor, so you can't be my friend." What there is is a kind of Venn diagram, those overlapping circles of who is who. And sometimes the girls who most perpetuate it have the least idea of what they're doing, you know? And they would be shocked if someone told them. As I say, these are nice girls, really nice girls. . . . I would send my own daughter here, if I had one, yes, I would. Although for faculty kids there's a whole set of different social issues. . . . So we're back to the Venn diagrams again.

11. June

"Stupid button," Hazel said, both hands searching backwards and blind so "Wait," I said, and reached it for her, the hidden hook-and-eye of the dress, a midnight blue halter dress, Alondra had loaned it to her. My own dress—an off-white Swee Jonson, sleeveless with a tulip skirt—was muggy with sweat; it had been so hot in the theater, Convocation had taken forever.

"I can't wait to get this thing off," I said, plucking at the neckline.

Outside was all the celebration babble, teachers, parents, everybody milling around under the lawn canopies, drinking mango punch and telling each other how phenomenal their kids were. My parents were there, and my Nana and Papa, Nana in sunglasses and a shell pink Panama hat, and of course Duncan and Magnus and "I can't believe Elbow," I said, even though I'd known Magnus was going to bring him, was determined to bring him, to smuggle him in if necessary. "Were you surprised?"

"Completely." Hazel dragged the dress up, muffling her

voice. "He was really good, though, wasn't he? He didn't bark until the end. Almost the end."

"Magnus told Mrs. Tai he was a therapy dog."

"Could there be a bigger lie?"

"It's not a lie. He's very therapeutic. . . . Are you going straight to the luncheon, or what? My Nana wants to sit with you."

"She's a sweetie. —Ah crap. Help," half snared in the dress, the bracelet snagging on the hem: the charm bracelet, my bracelet, her bracelet now. I unhooked that, too. She went into the bathroom, I lay back across her bed, crumpled Cherry Hot wrappers and half-folded sheets, and as she cleaned up, we talked: about the passings ceremony, where the senior class baton got handed on to the new seniors, and the orchestra played "Hymn to Sweet Unfoldings" while the First Scholars, senior and junior, got onstage, Julia in four-inch heels and this phenomenal blue-and-ivory tailored suit—it took four fittings, like a wedding dress—with poor Mike Lee behind her like an assistant, thin and nervous in his jacket and tie.

We laughed about Keisha's over-the-top Farewell— *Vaughn, make way for this junior class, because we're planning on making history!*—coming out in Keller's stoned-silly drawl; he was Keller, now, not Kells, and Auds was Audrey again, standing next to him, smiling up at him like a wife or something. We talked about Alondra's dress, a robin's-egg-blue Stella McCartney cut so low that you could practically see her whole boobs, Mrs. Alwin called it a cocktail dress and sent Alondra back to change or put on a wrap. About Mrs. Tai's freshly cut Frankenstein bangs, glued to her sweating forehead. About the four banner-carrying Vaughn Virgins, Hazel's own INDUSTRY catching the breeze like a sail, weighing "a lot more than you'd think, the stupid pole must be like ten pounds all by itself." We talked about nothing, really, and everything, the way we always did.

Finally "I'm roasting," I said, tugging again at my neckline, "I've got to get out of this thing. Save me a seat, all right?"

"Right between me and Nana," Hazel said. She popped on the pink aviator sunglasses. "God, don't you love that hat?"

"Remember about July," I said. "Ask Magnus, all right?"

"Stop asking me," she said. "It's not going to be a problem."

"Well, ask him anyway." She clicked her fingers at me, I stepped into the hall.

In my room, everything was still piled up on the floor, one big messed-up heap of bedding and clothes, shoes and textbooks, the gendarme and the Dirty Dolls, like Constance Brill used to do. Constance Brill. I hadn't thought of that name in months. . . . I tossed the dress on top of the pile, and showered, the coldest water the tap would give. Then I pulled on a toga skirt and my, Hazel's, Vaughn T-shirt, brushed back my hair, dabbed on lipstick, Juicy Girl Sun on Snow. Outside I could see the balloons, the flowers, the blue-and-ivory banner, CONGRATULATIONS floating with the breeze. In the mirror I saw a girl like a candle flame, glowing and pale.

"Congratulations," I said to her. "Now go and say good-bye."

12. May

They'd announced the results right before rehearsal, it was all anyone could talk about: next year's First Scholars. The junior girl was Julia Baumgarten, of course, but the boy was Mike Lee—actually Myung Lee, AP Physics and fencing—and not Patton Ponder after all. Julia tried to act as if she wasn't disappointed, as if she'd gotten exactly what she wanted, but you could tell she was furious. All through rehearsal she'd whispered and hissed to Audrey and Greer and Abby Feldman, the three of them clustered around her like an honor guard, until Mrs. Dixon finally told them to *Be quiet so we can concentrate, Julia, please! We only have today to do this!*

Sorry, Julia called back, her voice echoing up the theater aisle like Lady Macbeth's, tragic but strong. She'd been Lady Macbeth in freshman year; Patton had been Macduff. Zac Sklar was Banquo, he got so high at tech rehearsal that he fell offstage. I was the Second Witch, green face paint, plastic skulls braided into my hair: *By the*

pricking of my thumbs / Something wicked this way comes. . . .
It was actually pretty fun.

Rehearsal was theatrical but not fun, rehearsal wasn't
even technically necessary, since we went through Convocation every June and we all knew essentially what to do.
Before, when I was in lower school, they used to make the
upper school troop in across the lawns, but everyone com-
plained so much about the goose slime on their shoes that
now we just marched in from the theater parking lot. It
was all supposed to "flow," one class into another, but it
was usually more of a shuffling, stepping-on-the-back-of-
someone's-feet type thing. The seniors' commencement
was separate, so no one wore gowns or anything, just boys
in suits and girls in blue or ivory dresses. My mother was
trying to get me to go dress-shopping with her, just us
girls, *and Hazel too if you'd like, she's more than welcome to come
along.* My mother was trying extra-hard to be "support-
ive," to show me that my friendship with Hazel was fine
with her, since now she thought Hazel was going to keep
me at Vaughn, not lure me away. Right. . . . We'd fought
about it, that scene with my mother, or actually Hazel
fought with me, "gloves off," like Magnus said. I didn't like
to think about that day.

And ever since that weekend, I hadn't felt the same
about my mother. I kept seeing her in my mind, smiling
and smoking, patting Hazel on the knee: and all of it,
every second, was a lie. Lying to Hazel about liking her, ly-

ing to my dad about quitting smoking, lying to me about everything. . . . I could never say this to Hazel, but having a mother didn't mean having a good mother. Who knew what her own mom would have been like? A picture on the piano couldn't tell you anything. Actually Magnus was a better parent than anyone's parents I knew.

As Mrs. Tai's drone went on and on—*Remember the occasion, act the way a Vaughn girl acts*—I'd kept sneaking looks at my phone: eleven-thirty, eleven thirty-five, eleven forty-five, why was this taking so long? Except for Audrey and Kells, who would give the Sophomore Farewell that Keisha, a few rows back, was apparently still busy writing —the rest of us would stay in our seats almost the whole time anyway, our alphabetical seats. I was on the aisle, next to Jennifer Nethercut, who I knew slightly from swimming. Alondra and Essi were two rows ahead, since there were a million M's. Audrey, being Zhang, was all the way in the back.

And Hazel had been excused from this part of rehearsal, since she was outside learning to carry her banner, one girl from each upper class, REASON—KNOWLEDGE— INDUSTRY—SERVICE walking together gracefully without crashing their poles into each other, or letting the flag part touch the ground. Hazel called them the four horse-women: "Like Famine, Plague, and all that, except here it's anorexia, STDs, SATs, and—what's the fourth one?" But she was smiling when she said it, like a Bone joke told by Lady Vaughn.

"Which one are you again?" I asked, as we walked, finally, to the art room, Hazel carrying her vestal-head, blind white Styrofoam tucked under her arm and "I'm INDUSTRY," she said, making a face. "Like, uh, steel or something. Steely resolve. Steel-toed pumps. I should carry this head instead. . . . Do you want more gorp?"

"Yes," because I was starving, I'd already eaten half the bag. No time to go to the dining hall, not even to grab a piece of fruit; even though it was a half day there was still so much to do after rehearsal, too much. . . . Including packing up my room, or trying to: it was like a clown car in there, I couldn't believe I had so much stuff jammed into such a small space. The end of the year was always like that, that cooked-down, hurry-up feeling, trying to cram everything you had to do, everything you wanted to do, everything you'd planned to do, into these last few weeks.

Except this year. I mean, I did lots of things, most of them with Hazel, but all with this weird kind of behind-glass feeling, like I was—insulated. Or isolated. Like watching a meet in the natatorium from the hallway: you could see the water splash, but never feel it. It was like being in two places at the same time, or no place at all.

It was a crazy time anyway. Now that exams were over, everyone felt freer to go a little wild. Couples hooked up for the last time, or the first; people slipped out after curfew, smoked in the laundry rooms, sneaked in fireworks—bottle rockets, and another kind that made this horrible whistling noise, you could hear it across the whole campus. Alondra and Devi and some of the Korean girls had a midnight food fight in the common room, throwing cookies, spraying soda. The next day there were ants all over, Mrs. Alwin had a *fit*.

The seniors were practically gone already; all year, all they'd cared about was college, and now it was finally time. The juniors were delirious. And two freshmen, freshmeat, climbed on top of Kingfisher and unfurled a three-bedsheet banner, SOPHMORES ROCK! and everyone made fun of them for misspelling "sophomores."

And the real sophomores, my class, almost juniors now—it was kind of the best time, everyone said, the best part of Vaughn. Because the pressure of senior year was still in the future, but you were almost at the top of the ladder, a later curfew, more prestige; Hazel said it was like being the crown prince, all the perks and none of the work. . . . Hazel and Edward Flowers had celebrated the post-exam weekend by hooking up at the empty ice rink, in the equipment room: *Just like* Love Story, she told us. *The smell of hockey was everywhere, it was so romantic.*

Alondra had laughed. *Weren't you a little nervous? People go in there all the time, Mr. Haywood's always in there—*

Our love protected us, Hazel said; she laughed, too.

And all day, every day, people talked about summer, about their plans: vacation trips to Switzerland or San Francisco, internships and jobs. Alondra was going to work with a theater group in Boston, Keisha's parents were taking her to L.A. for some speaking class, Essi had an internship at a PBS station: *They call me "the prep,"* she said. *Not very PC, is it?*

And Hazel was going back to her old school, *Back to Bertram, can you believe it? Mr. Khalil set it up.* She was going to lead a kind of Urban Patterns project with some of their gifted-and-talented kids, making skits like the one she and Alondra and Essi had done. It sounded like fun.

The teachers were planning, too: Mr. Brown was taking new media classes; Ms. Bliss was going to Iceland. Ms. Holzer and her husband were going to the Poconos, a second honeymoon, even though they hadn't even been married that long. Some people said she wasn't going to teach at all anymore, because of the fertility thing. Ms. Nell was going to work through most of the summer, with the girls' swim team; she'd asked me again about joining. *You're a good swimmer, Lily, you could do very well.*

I thought of nightswimming. *It's a big time commitment,* I said.

She'd also sat me down to discuss my "options," a strained kind of conversation, like she was trying to be fair even though she absolutely disagreed with me. She laid out the pros and cons, while I sat trying to listen, to keep an open mind, even though they were her pros and cons, not mine. Like *Pro: the Vaughn family tradition,* which meant what, me turning into my mother? That's a pro?

But she did suggest other schools for me to look at, LeMieux for one, and Emmsler Academy; both of them were excellent schools, she said, either would be a fine fit for me but *How do you know that?* I'd asked, and I was serious: how could anyone tell what was right for me, what would fit me, when I couldn't even decide myself? Good teacher or not, she still couldn't see inside my brain. What *did* she see, sitting there tapping her waterproof pen against the tiles, in the smell of chlorine, the sound of the blowers, her swimming-world safe and secure: was that what school was supposed to be for, to tell you what you wanted? Who you were, or were supposed to be? But *They're just suggestions, Lily,* she'd finally said, half-smiling, half-sad. *Not answers.*

Because I was supposed to have the answer, my answer, especially by now, May, summer bearing down, Ms. Nell watching me splash my feet in the pool, watching the ripples reach the pool walls and bounce back, crisscrossing, confusing one another, making no pattern at all. I was supposed to put on my shoes, trot over to the Admin building, and say *I'm not coming back next year, because I'm going*—where? I didn't know. I didn't know why I never asked Hazel what she thought, why I avoided the subject with her totally, totally, totally, why when she asked about my summer plans I said vague things, or made jokes (*I'm thinking of enrolling Elbow in step class, he really needs to drop five*), or just shrugged. I didn't know what to do anymore except slip out at night to the river, breaking through the water weeds, shivering on the bank, towel over my head like a portable cave: alone. Completely alone, which was the—the peace of it, the peace of not being a Vaughn Virgin, or Lily Noble, or even Calla, of being totally no one for a little while, just a wet shape there in the dark.

I assumed I might get caught eventually, nightswimming, but in that distant way you think things that you don't really believe. So when it finally happened I was shocked. Sitting there dripping on the grass, head bent almost to my knees until *Hey!* a girl's voice, loud, scaring me to my feet. Tall and quick in a black T-shirt, for a second I'd thought she was Hazel, for a second we had just stared at each other kind of wildly: she had almost stepped right on me, she'd never seen me sitting there at all.

Then *Wow,* she'd said. Her voice was loud, with a kind of down-south accent, like Abby Feldman's but more liquid. *I'm sorry I stepped on you, did I step on you? You scared the hell out of me.*

Shhhh, I'd said, standing up; she was taller than me, younger than me. A freshman? She looked slightly familiar, but I didn't know her. I almost said What are you doing out here at four a.m.? but realized that it didn't matter, I didn't care, and it wasn't any of my business anyway. Who was I, Mrs. Alwin? So *Sorry I scared you,* I'd said instead, pulling the towel across my shoulders, turning for the evergreens.

Were you swimming? she asked, more quietly now, curiously. *In the river?*

Yeah.

Is that, like, allowed?

No.

Oh, she'd said, then *See you,* softly, walking away, one shadow blending into all the others, and I almost laughed, because that was the thing, that was what I told Hazel now, pushing at the art room door: "She *didn't* see me, right, she almost crushed my hand. . . . For a minute I thought she was you."

Hazel frowned. "Why didn't you tell me?"

"I just did."

"I mean before. About the swimming." She was looking at me oddly, a strange blank look like the blank white head under her arm, smooth Styrofoam stare and "I don't know," I said. "It wasn't like I was—hiding it, or anything."

"Well yeah, you kind of were. You never—"

"Girls," Mrs. Parais said, popping up from behind one of the worktables, "help me a minute, won't you?" to pile up the decoupage supplies: boxes of magazines, *Vogue* and *PK* and *Seventeen,* jars of gesso and Liquitex, a box of scissors and razor pens. While we worked, Mrs. Parais talked nonstop about the class portraits, how Mr. Morrison was having an awful time with the boys, how the lower school was doing favorite book characters again, the little girls were so cute in their costumes, Red Riding Hood, Raggedy Ann and "You could be the Little Mermaid," Hazel said to me, joking; was she joking? For once I couldn't tell.

She brought it up again at her birthday party, her Vaughn birthday party which meant me, Edward Flowers, Alondra, Essi, and Keisha taking over the common room, inhaling a praline cake Magnus had sent from Dean & DeLuca—

Alondra: "I think I'm getting high from all this sugar. That's not physically possible, is it?"

Keisha: "Shut up and cut me another piece."

—and watching Hazel open her presents, some choice swag, as Essi said. The girls got her a gift basket from La Coeur, the Sweet Tooth basket: instead of Tress Mud there was Cotton Candy Gel, and six lipsticks, and cinnamon body spray, we held Edward Flowers down and sprayed him, too. He gave Hazel a jokey present—a giant black-and-white stuffed dog that looked somewhat like Elbow, with a collar that said "Wobble," which was "Elbow" backwards, almost—but said her real present would come later, and we all said "Ooooh," and rolled our eyes as he grinned, and blushed a little, and Hazel laughed.

And I gave her a bunch of stuff: a pair of Blondy boots like mine, and a Juicy Girl lipstick set which she didn't really need, now, with that gift basket, and some other little things I thought she'd like. But my real present was a charm bracelet, my charm bracelet, fixed—modified—for Hazel. I'd taken off the heart-and-anchor charm, and the butterfly, but I left on *Finally 15*. And I added a red enamel cherry, for Cherry Hot, of course, and a tiny little flower, for me, Lily. And a wishbone, which she understood instantly, no one else did but no one else was supposed to, they all thought it was for good luck or something, for getting what you wished for. Even Edward Flowers thought that. But she knew it was for her, for Bone.

Since it was almost dinner by then, we went down past the tennis courts—everyone but Keisha, who had to go turn in her Convocation speech—to the little wild woodsy part between the courts and the duck pond, over by the teachers' housing but "No one's there now," Alondra said, "they're all in the dining hall," so we opened the beers we'd brought, two for Hazel and four for the rest of us, smuggled in, again, by Alonzo in honor of "HJT," we chanted softly as she drank: HJT, Hazel June Tobias, June for the month of her birthday, and June for her mother, she told me, beer on her breath, as we walked afterwards to the river, just Hazel and me together. "That's why I'm named that," she said, scuffling over a brick paver, her Chanel flip-flop fell off, she scuffed it back on. "Because she was June, too. June Tobias."

The sun was gold on the endless lawns, the flower beds alternating pinks and reds, roses and geraniums; Vaughn was so pretty, sometimes. Past the trees, the river shone like bronze. I said, "Why didn't you ever tell me that before?"

"Why didn't *you* tell *me*, about the swimming?"

"I don't— I didn't think it was that big a deal. I didn't think it was any kind of deal."

"Well, you're supposed to be able to tell me anything."

"I know. I do."

We sat down on the grass, in the damp heat of the shady trees, and I gave her her last present: the finger of Lady Vaughn with a ring on it, an infinity ring I'd braided myself, silver and green, wire and yarn. She laughed when she opened the box and saw the finger, then saw the ring and got quiet. It was so still, I could hear us breathing, a sound like the current in the river, like the whole year, everything we'd done and said, was all compressed into that one breath.

Then she burped, from the beer, a surprisingly loud and gross burp, and we laughed. Edward Flowers came down the bank just then, hands in his pockets. As we walked back toward the dorms, he and Hazel put their arms around each other, and she put her other arm around me. It was harder to walk like that than you'd think, we kind of swayed on the path, like one happy clumsy creature with too many arms and legs. As we got to the turn for Peacock, Edward Flowers asked me, "Would you ever date a fresh-meat, Lily? Just, you know, hypothetically."

"Why?"

He and Hazel looked at each other and shared a little smile. "No reason."

We stopped there, at the turn, we untangled ourselves. Two gardeners unspooled a massive yellow hose across the lawn. A long-haired girl zoomed past on a bike, a red tote hanging on her back. "It all depends," I said.

"On what?" Edward Flowers said.

"On if I'm hungry for fresh meat or not."

Hazel laughed, and pushed my shoulder. "Listen to her. She sounds just like me."

Stacey Nell

What I find so gratifying about teaching here—and coaching here, especially; I coach the upper-school girls' swimming and diving program—what I really love is the chance to be with these girls, and watch them become the people they're meant to be. I came here from a public school situation—it was a terrific school, in a large, affluent district, but what I never got there, and that I do get at Vaughn, is the chance to really get to watch the girls grow . . . That might sound like something out of a brochure, but the fact is it's true.

It isn't that they're all wonderful all the time, or that we don't have some rough patches, or that there aren't a few of them every year who, you know, kind of make me cringe. I mean, these are preteen, teenage girls, they're up to here with hormones, they're wrapped up in themselves and their lives. So you do get friction.

But what I see, consistently—and what I find the most amazing—is that these girls seek their own best way. Consistently. Even the ones you're not sure of, nine times out of ten they will surprise you. I've got one little gal on the team now, she's from a tiny little town in South Carolina, never swam competitively in her life, just horsed around in the local pool, and she's going to be one of my varsity stars next year. It isn't only that Vaughn gave her the opportunity to explore this talent in herself, this strength, it's that she chose to. She chose to take the opportunity. What else can we give to kids but the chance to make that choice, to use everything they've got? Everything they are?

There are always a couple, every year, who your heart just breaks for. You watch them struggle to find their way, you do whatever you can to guide them in the right direction—but then you let go. You have to let go. Because no one sees into your heart, you know, no matter how close you are, to a student, an advisee—in the end, you have to let go. Because what you want for her may not be what she wants for herself. And sometimes it's the girls you struggle the most to help who need your help the least. I've been surprised more than a few times by these girls.

13. September

"Corn shucks," Edward Flowers said, maneuvering around a waist-high stack. The ice rink lot was our crafting area, the whole decorating committee was there, Julia, Keisha, everybody walking around with hammers and fake flowers. "What is 'shucking' anyway?"

" 'Shuck' rhymes with 'suck,' did you ever notice that?" Chris Hepburn asked. He pushed his hair out of his eyes, it immediately fell back. "I love wordplay, don't you? Spell 'chrysanthemum' and win a prize, bud."

"M-U-M. And the prize, bud, is you get to tie *this* to *this*," the dangling ends of the banner to the back of the "hay cart" which was actually a partially disguised golf cart, FOLLOW ME TO MIXER! Welcome Back Mixer was in two days, the freshmen were supposed to have the hay bale maze constructed already but so far all they'd done was get hay stuck all over themselves, the girls were running around shrieking like preschoolers and "God," Chris said. Hair out of his eyes, right back in. "Who's up for freshmeat? Who's got a dart gun?"

"Is there any more of that wire twine?" Edward Flowers asked me. Even though I wasn't technically on the committee, he still wanted me to work with them, be with them. With him. He needed me now, I knew. "And those stupid scarecrow heads, did anybody see those?"

"They're in a bag by the pumpkins," Chris said. "A big blue bag."

I tugged on my sweatshirt, my old disintegrating LAMB hoodie; the breeze was turning cool. "I've got to go, Mrs. Parais wants me to help her sort tiles, or something. . . . Message me after dinner, OK? We'll do something."

"OK," Chris said, even though I'd actually been talking to Edward Flowers. Smiling up at me through his hair, his amazing smile that's mostly all eyes, just the smallest curve of his lips. "Bye, Noble. You look ultra-phenomenal in that hoodie, Noble, by the way."

"Thanks, Hepburn," I said. "You look ultra-phenomenal with that straw in your hair."

Edward Flowers made a face, pretending to be annoyed, but his eyes were so sad. I squeezed his shoulder and said "Don't dwell," knowing that he would know what I meant.

Hands in my pockets, I started back toward the classrooms, the art room, pavement to gravel, road to path: *You just have to find your path.* Magnus had said that to me once, more than once. The last time was at that café.

"Hey," someone called from behind, a girl's voice: Carla. "Lily, hey, where're you heading?"

"Art room."

"Walk with me? I'm going to swim practice." It had been Carla who'd caught me that night at the river, Carla who'd swum the river with me our very first week back, I'd dared her to do it even though *It's so gunky!* in her loud Carolina whisper, stepping like a stork through the reeds and the weeds. She ended up liking it as much as I did, maybe even more: *Because it's a secret, right? Our secret.* "You know you've got grass in your hair?"

"It's straw," I said. "We're making scarecrows for Mixer."

"You and Edward Flowers? And Chris Hepburn?" She raised her eyebrows. Her eyes were green-blue, like the water in the pool, turquoise. "So you're going?"

"To Mixer? Sure."

"With him?"

"Chris?"

"I meant Edward Flowers." And then she smiled, and I did, too.

At the natatorium she turned left and I turned right. "Say hi to Ms. Nell for me."

"Will do." Ms. Nell had her on varsity this year, the secret weapon. Ms. Nell had asked me, again, to try out for the team, but I'd said no thanks. She had also asked me about Hazel, although she didn't seem surprised, unlike pretty much everyone else: *Hazel Tobias didn't come back to us this year, did she?*

No.

Well. We'll certainly miss her energy. . . . Can I ask why you changed your mind? Because that *did* seem to surprise her, that I was back. I don't remember what I told her.

We'd planned the weekend on Convocation night: mid-July, Hazel's first week free of the internship, my first week back from my aunt's: We'll get together, we'd told each other. We'll get together the first weekend we can.

But almost from the minute I got there, Hazel waving at the airport—Hazel in her new short haircut, Hazel with her new wrist tattoo, no more charm bracelet—all she could talk about was Bertram. How fun the internship had been, all the kids had looked up to her. How weird but good it was to be back, meeting all kinds of people, girls she'd never noticed before like *Esther Grossman, and Shan Jacks. Shan is so funny, so deadpan, you know? She reminds me of, you know, Effi. I mean Essi.* Like Essi Lafamian was part of some fond but distant past, not a girl she'd hugged goodbye a little more than a month ago. *She called me a couple of times—Essi, I mean.*

Really? What'd she say?

I don't know, I haven't talked to her. I keep forgetting to call her back. I hadn't said anything, just stood watching Elbow trot around the dog park after an obese Jack Russell. We'd stopped there on our way to meet Magnus at some Italian place for lunch. *They're probably going to come over later,* Hazel said then, very casually. *Shan and Esther, I mean.*

It was like swimming in the river, when you hit a cold spot, cold even in the sun, the dry-baked dog-park runs and *I thought,* I said, staring at Elbow, *that this weekend was supposed to be just for us. I thought—*

Well, OK. We don't have to see them if you don't want to.

But she did want to, I saw that, felt it like an echo of everything she'd said and done since I'd come there, since she'd left Vaughn: the e-mails she hadn't answered, the jokes I hadn't heard, the slang words I didn't quite understand: *he's a huge suzie, it's so grillish.* It was like seeing her and not-seeing her, like seeing a ghost and that was when I knew, why without even thinking I said what I said: *You're not going to come back, are you? In the fall?*

She jumped, a little, but only a little. So she knew, too. *I— No. I don't know. I haven't made up my mind yet.*

The breeze, the barking, the cold. We weren't looking at each other, we were both watching Elbow. Finally she turned her head and *I never wanted to go there,* she said. She sounded mad. At what? At me? *It was all Duncan's idea.*

You—you led a tour. You carried a flag at Convocation. You loved the medieval-ness, you loved— A lot of things. Edward Flowers. And—

It's nice there, I'm not saying it's not nice. But I'm just—I'm not the Vaughn Virgin type, OK?

The metal fence behind me, holding me up. The bracelet on my wrist. *I was thinking of leaving,* I said.

Leaving Vaughn? You?

It was the way she said it, so—flat, so totally surprised,

as if Lady Vaughn had yanked her metal legs out of the ground and dashed off running, something impossibly unbelievable and strange. It was the truest thing either of us had said since I got there. *When were you thinking that?*

Never mind. It doesn't matter, now.

Seriously, when?

I said, it doesn't matter.

And then she looked away, not just not at me but away, toward the street, the traffic, the people passing, the guy swerving by on a bike. We stood like that for a long time, our backs pressed against the fence. Then she whistled for Elbow—who ignored her totally, she had to go scoop him up—and we walked eight blocks without speaking to meet Magnus at the sidewalk Italian place and eat Italian ices, sticky and slippery and cold. Magnus kept on glancing at me, at her, at me again, he'd known something was up. Finally, when Hazel went inside to use the bathroom, he'd leaned across the little round table, Elbow panting underneath and *She told you,* he said. It wasn't a question.

She didn't tell me, I said. *I asked.* Sweat trickled down my back, a salty ribbon. *Did she tell you?*

I knew.

I spooned up more ice, dark purple, almost black, black currant. It tasted like nothing, just ice on my tongue. *Did she tell Duncan?*

No, I did. He's furious. With utter relief. . . . But what about you, Calla?

And I'd looked down at the cold spoon, my cold hand,

feeling an empty soreness inside like a pulled splinter, a deep smooth splinter; was that relief? utter relief? and *I made up my mind*, I'd said to him. *I'm staying at Vaughn.*

Magnus looked at me hard then. He couldn't see my eyes behind my sunglasses, deep blue-onyx sunglasses, and I was glad. *You are? When did this happen?*

A little while ago.

Are you sure?

I'm sure, I'd said, because I was, because as soon as she'd said she wasn't coming back, I knew that I wasn't leaving. Emmsler and LeMieux, they might as well have been Vaughn anyway. And where else would I go? Bertram High? I—my mother would die. My mother would just die.

So you found your path, then?

Sometimes the path is a circle, who had said that? More ice on my tongue, numb. *Yes.*

Magnus seemed like he was going to say something else, I'd known he was going to say something else so *I'm all right,* I said then, to stop him. *I'll be all right.*

At the airport, Hazel hugged me goodbye, hugged me hard; her eyes were red. I had on my sunglasses and a Bertram T-shirt, so soft and new-smelling, she'd given it to me the night before. *Call me,* she'd said. *Call me a whole fucking lot.*

I will.

And tell people I said hi. But just the good people. Like E-flowers. Does he know? I wanted to ask. But I didn't. Of

193

course he didn't know. *Give him a hug for me. Just a hug, right?*

I smiled a little; she did, too. *Right.* Magnus waited on the sidewalk outside, by the cab. Duncan wasn't there. Or Elbow. *Walk Elbow for me, OK? He still needs to drop five.*

I will. . . . Bye, Calla.

Bye, Bone. *Bye, Hazel.*

Bone of my bone, flesh of my flesh, that's where the name comes from, why Duncan calls her that. It means, You are part of me, and I am part of you. To infinity. . . . I didn't really cry until the plane took off.

The art room looked empty, the overheads dimmed, but I could hear noises from the little storeroom, Mrs. Parais sorting through tiles, dozens of little multicolored ceramic tiles, she always started the year with mosaics because they were easy and hands-on: *Don't be afraid to dig in, girls.* Mosaics, then sisal weaving, then still-life drawing, then decoupage.

Lined up by the back wall were last year's vestals, all the best ones: Abby Feldman's, Devi Gupta's, Hazel's head-on-the-car. And mine, her bald body covered with symbols and signs, I NEED on her neck, on her lips the sideways 8, the line turning back in and around itself: infinity. I went up to her, my vestal, my Lady Vaughn, and slipped on her wrist the green-and-silver bracelet, Hazel's old bracelet, my bracelet. Infinity.

"Lily Noble?" Mrs. Parais called. She looked around, blinking, past the door frame. "Is that you?"

Like Edward Flowers says, Don't dwell. And I don't. I just wish she had been—different.

"It's me," I said. "I'm here."